BAKER'S DOZEN
Del Boland
with original lyrics and music by
Craig Christiansen

"Midnight
under the moonlight
Gazing up
at a starry sky
I'm wondering
if the world I know
is the world it seems . . . "

From 'I'll Never Understand You' by Craig
Christiansen
2014

MOON CREEK PUBLISHING FIRST EDITION,
APRIL, 2015

ISBN: 978-0-9915925-2-4

Book Design by Del Boland
Cover Design by Del Boland and Craig Christiansen

Printed in the United States of America

www.delboland.com
www.twitter.com/delboland
www.facebook.com/del.boland
www.goodreads.com/author/show/
8200106.Del_Boland

ACKNOWLEDGEMENTS:

To God, without whom, nothing is possible.

Anne, thank you for your support over the years. I'm lucky to have you.

Craig Christiansen, your music and your mission are an inspiration to me. Thank you for unlocking the potential in others.

Cousin Rebecca Hartman. Thanks for your expertise in stained glass. Yes. Marilyn can solder. ;-)

'Light Screens : The Leaded Glass of Frank Lloyd Wright,' written by Julie Sloan.

Al Kelkhoff. Who knew that a few days as a mixer guy could go this way?

"Uncle" Bud Tabaka. Thanks for your kind words and inspiration.

Lyrics and music from Craig Christiansen's compilation entitled Baker's Dozen are by permission of Craig Christiansen.

Dedicated to all the Baker's in my family; Harold, Tommy, Sheila, Barbara, Della, Nancy, Uncle James, Donnis, Maderia, and Pat.

CHAPTER ONE

"We start here." A midget clown slapped his leather riding crop against a paper map of downtown Chicago, a short cigar dangling from the lower corner of his sad mouth. He plucked near the hot end of the stump and threw it on the floor. Something scurried in the shadows.

Drew, his clown partner, scraped away from the table in a chair. Raising his lanky frame, he placed both hands flat and leaned over to get a better look at the map, bumping his bald head into a single lightbulb suspended by an ancient cord. The shadows shifted in the room as the bulb gently swayed in exponential decay. *Poink!* A drop of water echoed in the distance.

Standing on a wooden chair, Rex shook his disproportionately large head, rolling his eyes at Drew who stood motionless in clown shoes, sky blue leotards and a grossly undersized pink tutu. Above Drew's bulbous red nose, dark eyes winced in fear, despite painted eyebrows arched in perpetual surprise.

"Fix your cap," Rex said in a raspy voice, "it's down on one side."

Drew centered the rubber bald cap with wiry tufts of orange hair extending to either side, tugging around the edges.

Rex continued. "We work the neighborhoods then we hit Lincoln Park at lunch." He shifted his weight, exaggerating an angular motion through red shirt and suspenders to a wire ring on which hung dingy, black and white checkered pants.

"Hey, how 'bout the children's oncology ward?" Drew whined.

"That's our last stop. We'll take back streets," Rex growled, tracing the route with the leather crop.

"What if somebody sees us?"

"People will see us," Rex said. It's broad daylight."

"I know, but what if they get suspicious?"

"We'll be long gone."

CHAPTER TWO

A billowing, plastic grocery bag crinkled along the newly paved parking lot, tumbling past a light post in a wave of sunlight. *Windy. Clouds clearing and sunny in the afternoon.* Good.

Josh touched the screen of his cell phone, then placed it to his ear. He waited for the beep. "Dad, I'm at Music Universe. Just wanted to chat with you . . . hoping to get a little inspiration. Talk to you soon. Bye."

Standing on the driver's side of his Range Rover, he placed the phone back in his pocket. His cousin, John, had arranged for the meeting with the CEO and Kenny Ray.

Moments later, a white, stretch limo turned into the parking lot from the road, then slowed at the curb before stopping at the front door of Music Universe. A man in a suit, most likely the CEO, appeared in the vestibule of the store, motioning with his hand to the occupants of the car, inviting them inside. The driver's side door opened and a large, hispanic man in a chauffeur's uniform squeezed out then labored around the car. He opened the rear door. Kenny Ray emerged -- a black, flat brimmed, cowboy hat covering most of his shoulder length, blond hair. The slim guitarist turned in the direction of the parking lot where Josh stood next to his Range Rover. Josh waved. Kenny Ray tentatively waved back. His latest single, 'Texas Blacktop,' was number three and rising.

Several others filed out of the car behind the star, gathering at the entrance. The chauffeur waddled over and held the door for Kenny Ray and his entourage to enter.

Showtime.

Josh opened the back glass of the Range Rover, retrieving his tweed guitar case and his latest amp design, a Blues Eight. The black Tolex covering and brown grill cloth with gold thread stitched into diamond shapes had a vintage look, but the circuitry was solid state. He'd cracked the code for producing vintage tones in a tubeless amplifier. Lightweight and virtually maintenance free, it offered a range of tones previously unavailable at the consumer end of the market. He needed exposure.

Josh carried the amp and his guitar case to the open front door of Music Universe where Bob, the store manager, now stood waiting.

"He's here," Bob said.

Josh nodded. "Yeah, I saw him."

"No, my boss." Bob shifted his medium build, glancing over his shoulder.

Josh smiled reassuringly. "Relax, it's gonna be fine."

"That's easy for you to say. The CEO never visits the store."

Bob looked at the Blues Eight then at Josh's guitar case. "Where's the amp?"

"This is it."

"Where?"

"Here." With little effort, Josh lifted the amp to chest level.

Bob's eyes widened. "Are you kiddin' me? That's the amp that's gonna revolutionize the industry?!"

"Don't sell it short until you hear it."

Bob said, "It looks like a practice amp." He glanced over his shoulder again, then turned and smirked. "My boss is inside with the hottest guitar player since John Mayer, and you're here with a practice combo?!"

"Relax," Josh said. "When you hear it, you'll understand."

"Kenny Ray plays large venues." Bob sniffed. "These amps don't have the headroom or the tone at high levels, even when miked."

"Trust me, okay?" Josh said. "It'll respond. It's built into the design of the circuit."

Bob exhaled loudly. "If it wasn't for your cousin, I'd pull the plug on this whole thing."

Josh smiled. His cousin, John, knew Chuck Weinstein, CEO of Music Universe.

Bob stepped aside, bracing his body against the door for Josh to enter the vestibule. Inside,

Bob grabbed his arm. "You owe me big time for this, Josh Baker."

"I'll make a deal with you." Baker smiled. "If I deliver, then you help me with my next big project."

Bob glanced inside the store through the glass door. "You're on. Don't screw it up."

"Thanks for the inspiring words."

Bob sighed, then opened the second door for Josh to pass, inviting an assault of amplified guitar sounds into the small space in which they stood. Inside, two teenage boys played familiar phrases through demos in dissonant contrast to a recording of Stevie Ray Vaughan's 'Stang's Swang.' Josh cringed. "How do you *stand* it?"

"What?"

"All this noise," Josh said.

"What noise?"

Josh shook his head.

Seventy or eighty guitars hung on the large, back wall of the store. Arranged to either side, amplifiers, PA systems, drums, lights, keyboards . . . paradise.

Bob, waved at Kristin, his assistant, who approached from the Drum Department. "Where *are* they?" he said.

Kristin waved timidly at Josh before responding. "The freak show's in the back. I see nothing. I know nothing."

"Go kill the music," Bob said, motioning to Kristin before turning and walking toward the rear of the store. "Alright, hotshot," he shouted over his shoulder, "don't embarrass me."

Josh weaved around a display, nearing the group of demo amps where the two boys continued playing. Stooping, Josh set his guitar case down. One of the boys -- a kid with acne -- glanced at him. Josh nodded encouragement then placed his amp on top of a Fender Bassman combo. The two aspiring guitarists joined forces, attempting a Zeppelin cover.

Fishing a cord and a footswitch from the back of his amp, Josh knelt, placed the controller on the floor and opened his guitar case. He lifted his vintage '57 Stratocaster and ducked under the strap.

The boy with acne stopped playing and motioned to his older companion who paused. "Whoa," the older boy said -- both gawking at the relic resting on Josh's knee.

He stood, plugged both ends of the cord, and began tuning the guitar, watching the meter clamped to the headstock display green for each string.

The house music abruptly stopped in the middle of a guitar solo, a momentary silence interrupted by voices echoing from the rear of the store, slowly approaching. Josh waited.

The younger boy gazed in the direction of the men rounding the corner from the stockroom. Mouth agape, he poked his friend. "Look," he whispered, "it's Kenny Ray."

Bob led the tour -- a game show host, smiling and waving his arms ceremoniously.

"Gentlemen, I'd like you to meet Joshua Baker," Bob said. "Josh has a new product."

Josh nodded at the group, now standing six feet away. A guy in faded jeans and a Kenny Ray concert tee looked at the little amp and chortled, "That's it?! That's what you wanted to show us?"

Kenny Ray flashed a Hollywood smile at the group, then turned to Josh. "Let's hear whatch'a got," he said with a drawl.

Josh pressed the first switch on a floor controller and struck an E chord. The six men flinched then shuffled back a few steps as the chord sustained, producing a warm, saturated tone, much like a vintage Fender blackface. Josh stepped on another switch then played a few standard Hendrix chops.

Kenny nodded his head with approval.

Josh selected a third switch from the controller and played a clean tone with some reverb mixed in. He played a 12 bar New Orleans shuffle, then moved into a rendition of Kenny Ray's hit single, "Texas Blacktop."

"Nice! You mind?" Kenny Ray asked.

"Not at all." Josh used a thumb to lift the strap over his head, freeing himself, then presented the Strat to the young guitarist who held it up, examining it carefully before strapping it on. Kenny switched places with Josh, moving closer to the foot controller, exploring the fretboard with the volume turned down. Nimbly, he used his pinky on the volume knob, then ripped a blinding phrase through the amp, picking each note cleanly -- more of a Nashville sound. He switched the 5 way to the front two pickups, then pressed the first switch on the foot controller. He launched into the signature lick of a familiar song from his first album, producing a muted, hollow tone through the Stratocaster.

"Whoa!", mouthed the boy with acne.

Kenny Ray alternated between switches while demonstrating his range of styles, moving from Hendrix to Vaughan to Carlton.

The star turned down the volume, lifted the strap over his head and handed the guitar back to Josh. "I'll take two."

Josh turned to Bob. "I . . . uh . . . I only brought this one."

"Give 'im a card, George," Kenny Ray said. "Just ship the other one. I'll take this one."

George, a cleanly shaved man wearing a button down Oxford shirt and pin striped slacks, cleared his throat. "Hold on a second, Kenny." He turned to Bob. "How much?"

Bob, still smiling from ear to ear, leaned close so only Josh could hear him. "How much you asking for this thing?"

"I need to make $375.00 for each unit," Josh whispered.

Bob turned to George. "That'll be $1,550.00 for the two amps. We'll pay shipping."

"No problem."

Bob turned back around, still grinning.

"Ask him," Josh said.

"Ask him what?"

"About an endorsement."

"Let him use the amp on stage, then ask for the endorsement."

Bob was euphoric. He'd scored in front of his boss who now led Kenny Ray and the entourage to a cash register.

"Hey, don't forget about our deal," Josh said.

"What deal?"

Baker sighed. "You said you'd help me with my next big project."

Bob's smile faded. "Josh, you need to focus on your current project. Let's take it one step at a time."

CHAPTER THREE

A girl squealed on a merry-go-round at Wicklow Park, bracing herself as a freckle faced boy ran in a circle along a deep rut. His legs unable to keep up, he jumped aboard, feeling the centrifugal force pushing him outward. A barely audible, yet familiar sound drew his attention.

He leapt from the spinning mass, hurling himself at a full run toward the corner of the park, abandoning the girl.

In the distance, through waves of heat rising from the pavement, a panel truck lumbered steadily toward the playground, playing an incessant xylophone version of 'Do Your Ears Hang Low.'

The boy waited for the approaching van -- two clown occupants bouncing along inside -- until it crossed the intersection. *Go!* He ran along the grassy edge of the park, racing -- human versus machine -- until the truck slowed to a stop ahead of him, the song still blaring. Gasping, he trotted to the end of a line of kids who'd gathered along the curb.

A thin clown in blue appeared in the window on the side, smiling.

Juan, a first grader at the front of the line, said, "I want a grape snow cone."

The kids giggled as the midget clown's head bobbed across, just above the opening. The little man's upper body rose stepwise, reaching a height from which he leaned closer to three glass dispensers, each with colored flavoring. He pumped grape juice on the top of crushed ice mounded above the rim of a paper cone.

"That'll be $1.50," the thin clown said, taking Juan's money in exchange for the treat.

Just like all the other ice cream vendors around Chicago, they rounded their prices to the nearest quarter, keeping it simple for themselves and the kids. All the other vendors paid sales tax out of their total sales. Rex and Drew paid no tax.

CHAPTER FOUR

A sign taped to the door read:

LIVE MUSIC!
TONIGHT: THE FALLO WING

"Come on down, it'll be like old times," Darius had said.

Josh pushed the door open and stepped into the dimly lit tavern, feeling a thrust of music from the stage.

" . . . And so it's sad to say, there may never come a day", Tom Osborne belted mid song, "that we can live in peace and love and harmony . . . all across the seven seas."

Several patrons watched the band from two tables nearby. On stage, Austin nodded at Josh from behind his drums, then twirled a stick without missing a beat in front of their banner which hung loosely on a brick wall behind him -- a mangled wing forming the letter F and another half extended wing span forming a capital W in 'The Fallow Wing.'

Near the bar, a few locals faced a large, flat screen television mounted on the wall -- the Cubs and the Braves. The smell of beer and fresh pretzels reminded Josh that he'd not eaten.

" . . . set me free, can't you see, that we're in control of you and me," Tom sang with his red, Epiphone 335 copy strapped at an angle in a defiant stance.

Stringy brown hair hanging over his face, Tom launched into his solo, leaning over with the guitar pointed at the stage. He shuffled in canvas shoes across the stage . . . heels, toes, heels, toes. A drunk girl at one of the tables shouted, "Woo hooo! Yeah!"

For the first time, Josh began to appreciate the full impact of Tom's stage presence as part of the audience. As a member of the band, Josh had always taken a position on the opposite side of the stage from Tom, facing forward. Tom's look was right. The chops were right. The attitude was right, but his guitar tone needed tweaking.

On stage, a shapely blonde woman in a white evening gown stood between a set of congas and a keyboard, playing maracas and singing harmony on the chorus. He'd not seen her before.

Funkmaster Darius thumped a forefinger against the E string of his Precision bass next to the drums, playing in the pocket, his head -- sporting a black, pork pie hat with the brim rolled up -- bobbing with the beat. Together, he and Austin were the best all around rhythm section in town, having played together in a number of other groups. They knew every nuance, every turnaround, every shuffle to every song written since the 30's.

Tom played the song's signature lick before ending the song.

"We're gonna take a break," Darius said into his mike. "Hang around. We've got a special treat for you." He grabbed a pink fuzzy cloth from the top of his amp, wiped his strings, then unstrapped the bass and put it on a stand.

Josh stepped up on the stage and grabbed Darius by the hand, chest bumping him, their clasped hands pinned between them. "What's up?" Josh said.

"Don't 'what up' me, cracka! Where've you been?"

Austin smiled, now standing behind his vintage pearl white Ludwigs, arms folded, sticks in one hand.

"Who's the girl with the maracas?" Josh said, tilting his head quickly over his left shoulder.

"Oh, that's Marilyn." Darius grinned. "She *do* have some nice ma*rac*as," he said, nodding as he spoke.

Austin laughed. "You can for*get* it, brother," he said with a slow drawl. He lowered a hand and fished something from the back pocket of his faded jeans.

Josh said, "What?"

"I've seen that look before," Austin said. "She ain't your type." He opened a tin can, pinched some snuff and poked it under his lower lip.

"Yeah, she's from Bonni-rich-whitey-ville," Darius said.

"You ever been to Bonniville?" Josh asked.

"*Naw*, man."

"It's really nice," Josh offered, still eyeing the girl.

Austin laughed through a bulge in his lower lip.

"Josh!" Janie waved from the bar. Her dark, pixie cut hair accentuated her slender neck -- a modern day Audrey Hepburn. Josh waved. "How's she doing?"

"You never know," Darius said. "She's between boyfriends."

Janie tossed the last of her beer back, placed the empty glass on the bar, then walked toward Josh with arms open. He stepped down and embraced her, then held her narrow shoulders at arm's length. "Wow. You look *great*," he said, admiring her sultry smile.

Janie winked at him. "Watch out," she said, "here comes the ice queen," motioning with her sparkling gold eyes.

The blonde in the evening gown had stepped down from the stage. Austin said, "Josh, this is Marilyn Gustafsson." She held a slender arm out with her hand drooping slightly from the wrist. Josh took it. She smiled like a contestant at a beauty pageant, her hair up in a braided bun.

"Yo brutha! Leggo dat woman 'fore she put a *spell* on you," Darius said in his comical street voice -- a contrast to his otherwise straight up, GQ persona.

Marilyn angled her eyes toward Darius then turned and sauntered across the dance floor to a table where Tom sulked, playing his guitar, looking down at a sheet of paper. "What's up with *him*?" Josh asked.

"Aw, he's still mad 'cause you quit the band," Austin said over his bulging lip. "So, why'd you quit the band?"

"I told you, I can't do the road thing."

Austin rolled his eyes. "Whatever."

Several folks cheered as a Cubs player hit a double into right field.

"We're going outside," Darius said. "Wanna take a ride?"

"No thanks, I'm fine."

Austin said, "Mr. Goody two shoes, always takin' a pass."

Janie followed Darius and Austin to the front door.

Josh checked the score on the screen, 3-2 Braves. He turned and wandered over to Tom's table.

"How's the amp business?" the Aussie, Tom, asked without looking up.

"Not great."

Tom scribbled something, then played a chord and sang a line. Marilyn nodded her approval.

"I heard you moved to tha warehouse," Tom said, glancing up for a moment, round glasses resting on the slight crook of his long, thin nose. He brushed his shoulder length, stringy brown hair over one ear then looked back down, writing again.

"Yeah," Josh said.   "It's actually a nice neighborhood."

The crowd booed at the runner tagged out trying to steal third.

Josh tilted his head, trying to read the words but Tom's arm surrounded the paper, protecting his work. "Whatcha writin'?"

"Revisin' a song."

Josh forced a crooked smile.   "If you'd like some help with your amp," he said, "I'm happy to share what I know."

"I loik it just the wye it is."

Josh nodded.   Marilyn angled her eyes in his direction.

Josh said, "Some of the Deluxe Reverbs from the 60's had a feedback suppression circuit."

"Yee-uh, so I've been told," Tom said. "I loik the clane sound."

Josh checked himself. He wasn't boasting, but rather, simply offering help to a fellow musician.

She tilted her head, still watching him.

Josh said, "Yeah, me too." Tom resumed his work.   Josh continued, " . . . but it's nice to have some natural overdrive and sustain, especially for solos."

Tom looked up again. "Oi'm good."

Marilyn said, "Darius wants you to get up for a few songs."

"I know," Josh replied, "but I just sold my amp."

Tom drummed his pen against his cheek, still looking down. "You can use moin," he said, "if you kin stand the rotten tone."

"That's okay," Josh answered. "I'll take a pass. I'd rather hear you guys play anyway."

"I was wonderin' why you kime without the Strat," Tom said.

"It's out in the car."

Tom said, "I don't thank that's woise."

Josh surveyed the crowd. "It's fine."

Marilyn's lips turned up slightly at the corners, revealing her dimples. "You can sit down if you want," she offered, pointing at an empty chair.

He pulled the chair and ordered a Diet Coke from the waitress who'd delivered a glass of white wine to Marilyn and a beer to Tom.

Josh felt relieved for the company as he waited on the others to return, pretending to watch the game. Maybe he'd tag along after the show. Maybe she'd go, too. What better way to get acquainted?

The crowd groaned as a Cubs pinch hitter struck out swinging.

The door creaked open. Two office women laughed as they entered with a nicely dressed man, followed by Darius, Janie and Austin. The three bumped playfully into each other, weaving between tables. Janie scraped a chair along the wooden floor next to Josh.

With a wry grin, Tom said, "You mie wanna sty downwind of the jacks." Janie giggled. Marilyn lips parted, revealing her straight white teeth.

Did she smile at me?, Josh wondered. She seemed calm and content, her long fingers resting comfortably on the table.

Austin signaled the bartender who turned the sound down on the television. "On in two," he said, spitting into a styrofoam cup before swigging his beer.

Standing behind Marilyn, Darius bent his 6'2 body at the waist to each side. "Basketball's takin' a toll," he said, straightening.

Austin swigged the last of his beer, and placed the empty bottle on the table. "Time to make the donuts," he said. He wandered across the dance floor, then stepped onto the stage, Darius following close behind. They milled around for a minute before taking their places -- part of their routine.

With a nod from Darius, they began the next set with a bass and drum groove, warming up for Tom. Marilyn stood then sashayed to the stage, finding her spot behind the keyboards. She opened a case, pulled out a harmonica, blew through it, then adjusted her mike stand.

Josh replayed the scene in slow motion . . . Marilyn puckering her lips and blowing on the harp. He shook the image from his mind.

Baker's Dozen

Darius and Austin finished their instrumental opening as Tom, with his guitar strapped around his neck, mounted the stage holding his beer. He placed the nearly full glass on a stool then plugged his guitar, playing a few chords.

"Here's a little song I wrote," he said. "It's called "Killing Ourselves"."

KILLING OURSELVES
(Track 5)

Every day
in every way
we're killing ourselves,
killing ourselves baby
every night,
with every light
we're killing ourselves,
killing ourselves baby
look up into dingy skies
with tired apathetic eyes

More gas tanks
more loans to the banks
we're killing ourselves,
killing ourselves baby

Del Boland

Oily seas,
toxic breeze
we're killing ourselves,
killing ourselves baby
pesticidal
genocide
we're killing ourselves,
killing ourselves baby

I hope that we don't
want to be remembered
as a selfish generation
that borrowed from tomorrow
in every single way
and cannot repay it

Populate
radiate
we're killing ourselves,
killing ourselves baby
busy streets,
hormonal meats
we're killing ourselves etc.

CHAPTER FIVE

From the empty dance floor, Josh eyed a waitress turning chairs upside down on tables.

"So, when do I get to see the warehouse?" Janie asked. He angled his gaze at her, playing coquettishly with the tasseled beads on her cheesecloth top.

He glanced over his shoulder at the stage as Marilyn, Darius, Tom and Austin busily packed their gear behind Janie.

Loud enough for the others to hear, Josh said, "Yeah. Uh . . . maybe the others would like to come over *too*." Marilyn zipped a cover on her keyboard near Tom who shook his head, glaring at Janie from his kneeling position onstage. Austin scowled, rapidly shaking his head no. Darius cut his throat with his finger.

Still facing Josh, Janie smiled wryly. "They're all making faces, aren't they?"

"Yeah, kinda," Josh said. "Maybe you can follow me in your car."

"I'm not driving these days," she said.

"Oh."

CHAPTER SIX

Josh turned onto Randolph.

In the passenger seat, Janie hugged her knees, her face resting on top, turned toward him. She studied his cleanly trimmed beard. "You've always reminded me of Kenny Loggins."

"Thanks," Josh said.

The tire noise shifted briefly from a whine to a roar as they crossed the Chicago River bridge. Headlights approached from the opposite lane, whooshing by -- a car making its way toward the loop.

"Where are we?" Janie asked, eyeing the dark, passing outlines of warehouses.

"Fulton Street Market."

"Aren't you afraid?" she said.

Josh laughed. "It's mostly residential. Developers are converting the warehouse buildings to lofts."

"Oh," she said. "How much is an old warehouse building worth?"

Josh bit his lower lip, then said, "I don't know. My dad's building needs work." He lifted his blinker, slowed, then turned. "Hard to say, really. The taxes are ridiculous."

"Why don't you sell it?"

Josh glanced at her.

"It means a lot to my dad," he said. "He built his business from scratch."

The SUV slowed, then turned again, the headlights coloring the side of a brick building before coming to rest on a metal door. Josh reached up and touched something on his visor. Wan light washed over the hood of the Land Rover as the garage door lifted, revealing the interior of a high bay warehouse. Josh eased into the open space, then touched the button on his visor again, closing the door behind them.

They rumbled slowly across a black, woodblock floor toward the back wall. Josh carefully maneuvered the SUV next to a decked out Harley Davidson Superglide, then stopped. He shifted into park and unlatched the door, a *bing boong* noise reminding him to remove his keys. "C'mon, I'll show you around," he said, exiting the driver's side.

Janie turned and slid from the tan leather seat onto the ground, following him into the open space.

"Harvey!" Josh shouted. "I want you to meet somebody!"

An enormous, crewcut man walked toward them from a shop area, one corner of his bib overalls strapped over a hairy shoulder, exposing one side of his barrel shaped chest.

"Dude, you finally snagged one!" he teased, pointing at Janie, his stubbled face grinning at Josh.

"This is Janie. We've known each other for years."

"Welcome to the psych ward," Harvey said, extending a hand

"Hi."

Harvey held her hand in the same way most folks would hold a twig, wrapping his fingers all the way around.

The initial whine of an electric motor, followed by a loud whirring noise startled Janie. Fifty feet behind Harvey, wearing denim cargo pants and a red flannel shirt with sleeves rolled to the elbows, a muscular woman glared from the shop area -- a red bandana over her short brown hair. She lifted an ax slowly then pressed it against a rotating wheel, skittering sparks into the air.

"That's Rosie." Harvey said. "Don't worry, she's mostly harmless. Just don't get too close."

Janie hummed a song she sang as a child. Her father's voice sang out to her, "I know you're in here somewhere." She giggled from inside her favorite hiding place -- an old cedar wardrobe -- always the last place he looked. *Boomp. Boomp, boomp.*

A deep, pulsating noise grew increasingly louder, thumping around the outside of the building until it stopped near the lifting garage door, revealing large tires, then headlights shining into the space from a panel van. Rap music pounded as the van moved forward, the garage door closing behind it.

Glaring headlights obscured the dark occupants until the panel van neared them. Through the open door, a thin clown sat tall in the driver's seat, driving slowly past with a midget clown passenger. Along the side, BIG TOP MUNCHIE TRUCK emblazoned the top -- written in circus style letters. An assortment of food images were arranged below the letters, including an ice cream cone, a Chicago style hot dog, a bratwurst, snow cones, cotton candy and a pop -- all inside a painted wooden frame resembling a circus wagon.

The van pulled around the Land Rover, partially obscuring their view. The top of the passenger door slid shut. Janie waited, clutching her bag, her head slightly tilted.

At once, two clown heads -- one grinning and one frowning -- popped out horizontally around each end of the Land Rover. Their heads slowly retracted from her view, behind the parked vehicle. Within seconds, the two clowns marched from around the SUV -- the frowning, midget clown wearing a black top hat in the lead, and the goofy smiling clown close behind. They walked in exaggerated military style across, then abruptly turned ninety degrees, marching in line toward Janie -- demonstrating their great difference in height. The midget clown stopped abruptly and the taller clown fell over him, smashing his crushable, stovepipe hat. The shorter clown pantomimed his frustration, using his crushed hat to swat the taller clown who cowered in fear.

"Okay you clowns," Josh said, grinning, "this is Janie." He pointed at the short clown who waddled over. "Janie, this is Rex, our sound engineer and resident cook with an unauthorized food truck on the side . . . *ahem*!"

"My pleasure missy," he said with a rasp, holding his pancaked hat against his chest and bowing.

"And this is Drew," Josh continued, "who's also our accountant."

"Nice to meet you, ma'am." Drew drawled, also bowing.

Staring at Rex, Harvey scratched the exposed side of his hairy chest. "What've I told you about parking near my bike?"

Rex jerked his oversized head in Harvey's direction. "You might want to invest in some decent clothes, Neanderthal Man," he sneered.

"You've got a lot of room to talk, fruit loops."

Josh held both hands up. "That's enough, guys."

His hands still raised, Josh motioned with his head to Janie. "Let me show you around."

She followed. Mostly empty except for a few pallets of shrink-wrapped cardboard boxes, the shadowy, open space of the warehouse reminded Janie of an abandoned mill from a music video. Ahead, at the opposite end of the rectangular space, a light covered by a China hat on a gooseneck conduit illuminated a mezzanine -- surrounded on three sides by offices.

"So, you actually *live* here?"

"I do now." Josh bent over and picked up an empty beer can. "Actually, we *all* live here."

He tossed, rattling the can into a 55 gallon drum resting near a dusty brick wall with peeling beige paint.

They approached steel steps leading to the mezzanine. Janie hesitated. Josh stepped up one step, then reached for her hand. "It's okay, just follow me." She took his hand, walking very closely behind until they reached the top.

As Josh used a key to open a door, a scratching noise drew Janie's attention to the other side of the platform. Someone moved out of the shadows. A slender, black man stood, watching from across the mezzanine. "Oh my *God*!" Janie screamed, grabbing Josh.

"It's okay. That's just Freddie."

"*Freddie!*" Janie half whispered, eyes wide. "Are you *kidding* me?!"

She followed Josh into a dimly lit corridor. He opened a door and felt along the inside wall for a light switch, flipping it. Fluorescent lights flickered on inside a room, revealing a cozy living area arranged against the far wall. End tables with lamps and dark leather chairs flanked a matching couch on blue, office grade carpeting speckled with tiny gray and tan squiggles. Against the near wall down to their right, a conference table sat dormant, surrounded on three sides by office chairs and a few stacked on top.

"Can I get you anything?" Josh asked.

"How about a glass of wine?"

"I'll be right back."

Janie wrapped her arms around herself and began rocking gently back and forth. Her father's face smiled in front of her, getting closer then further away. The wind blew her pink dress around her legs which extended in front of her. Blue sky . . . daddy . . . daisies . . . daddy . . . blue sky. She lifted high into the air and felt the weight of her body as she descended, swinging happily.

"Janie?"

Her mother called to her.

"Janie? Are you okay?" Josh held a glass of white wine.

"Oh. Yes. I'm fine," she said, taking the glass and gulping it down. She placed the goblet on an end table then wrapped her arms around herself again, rocking and humming softly.

"Would you like me to take you home?" Josh asked.

Janie slipped a hand from the crook of her arm to wipe under one eye.

"Are you sure you're okay?" Josh asked again.

She sniffed and wiped under the other eye. "I'm kinda between homes right now."

"Oh no," Josh said. "I'm sorry."

"It's okay. I'm just a little freaked out at the moment."

Josh sighed. "I should've warned you."

"No, really, I'm okay."

"Why don't you stay here tonight? You can stay in my room and I'll sleep here on the couch."

"Um . . . " Janie sniffed then glanced around the room. "Okay."

Josh moved slowly to her, gently wrapping his arms and holding her. She nestled her head against his warm chest.

He held her for a minute, then spoke softly. "Let me get you some pajamas."

"Okay." He moved gently away from her then weaved around the conference table which partially blocked a doorway.

Janie peered at his dark image through the opening. A lamp clicked on. He walked away from a bedside stand toward a chest of drawers, retrieving two pairs of folded pajamas. Weaving back around the conference table, Josh offered her the top set of PJ's. "They may be a little big."

Superman pajamas?, she thought. What grown man has Superman pajamas?

"They were a gag gift," Josh said.

"What?"

"The pajamas." He nodded toward the door. "Go in and make yourself at home. I've got a pillow and a blanket here in the closet."

"Thank you." Janie leaned into him, lifting on her toes, kissing him on the cheek. She grasped his hand, but stepped away, holding it briefly before letting her fingers slip. She stepped through the opening, then pushed the door partially closed behind her.

Seconds later, she peered through the crack, her golden eyes sparkling beneath dark bangs. "Josh?"

"Yes."

She said, "I'd feel a lot better if you'd stay in here with me."

He seemed oddly hesitant. She'd never seen him with a girlfriend. Maybe he's gay, she thought.

"Okay. Let me change and I'll be in there in a minute."

Janie closed the door, then walked to a chair, noticing her reflection in a full length mirror. She removed her smock top and jeans, viewing herself in tattered panties. Feeling her noticeably protruding ribs, she winced at her shrunken breasts. Janie quickly slipped into the oversized Superman pajamas then padded across the carpeting. Pulling back the covers on one side of the bed, she slid between perfectly smooth sheets.

She took a deep breath, then tugged the covers up over her neck and chin and surveyed the room. She thought, at one time, the room must've been an executive's office, with hardwood paneling on the walls. A dresser with a television and a mirror sat opposite from the bed, close to the door leading to the living area. On one side, the chair with her jeans, top and bag. On the other side, the full length mirror. Another door led back out to the corridor. Janie hoped that a third door between the bed and the chest of drawers led to a bathroom. She'd wait to find out.

A moment later, Josh emerged wearing red and black plaid pajamas. "The bathroom's in there." He pointed to the third door.

"I'm okay for now."

He stepped into the restroom.

Her father's heartbroken face stared at her from across a hospital bed in the ICU. A droning *eeeeeeeeeeeeeeeee*. Disinfectant.

"Can I turn out the light," Josh said from the opposite side of the room. "Um . . . sure," she said. He'd combed his mid length, brown curly hair. She wondered how long he'd been there.

He turned off the overhead and his feet shuffled across the floor, faint light painting an orange path across the carpet from the bathroom. The bed moved as he pulled the covers back and gently lay on the other side.

She wanted to feel him close to her again. She wanted to feel his warmth radiating into her body. She needed his safety at that moment.

"Good night," he murmured.

"Good night."

CHAPTER SEVEN

Through the glass, white uniformed workers slid assembled amplifiers into plastic bags then lowered them into boxes fitted with molded styrofoam. One man pressed a final piece of styrofoam snugly over the amplifier before laying a clear plastic packet containing the owner's manual on top, then closing the lid and taping it. The finished boxes moved down a conveyer where they were systematically stacked and shrink wrapped on a rotating palletizer.

"And, this is our final packaging and shipping line," Royce Jacobsen said.

Josh put a finger inside his collar and tugged.

Jacobsen narrowed his eyes. "Not used to the suit and tie?" he asked.

"No. Not really," Josh admitted. "I prefer loose, comfortable clothing."

"Yeah, we don't have too many hippie types here at Magma Electronics."

One of Jacobsen's VPs snickered.

The CEO extended his hand to one side. "Let's go to the conference room."

Three men, also in suits, followed their boss through a door, then down a hall where awards, pictures of executives, and engraved brass replicas of patents adorned the wall.

Mr. Jacobsen stopped outside of an opening on the right and waited for his VP's and Josh to file inside a room with cherry paneling. The men arranged themselves near high backed chairs around one end of a long table.

"Please sit down," Jacobsen said, standing tall at the front of the room. He pointed a remote at a projector mounted from the ceiling and the machine whirred to life. He turned and separated two cherry paneled pocket doors, revealing a screen, then faced them.

"Mr. Baker," he said boldly, "Magma Electronics has been in business for 74 years. We began making radios before World War II and branched into what is now several divisions, including this building, which is part of our Music Products Division."

Appearing on the screen next to him, the Magma Electronics logo with a red M and E inside a black circle over a background lightning bolt. Mr. Jacobsen advanced to the next slide. "As a company traded on the New York Stock Exchange, we report our monthly earnings to the analysts who help valuate our stock. As you can see, we've doubled in size over the past two years, despite the difficult economy."

A graph showed a steady increase.

He advanced the slide. "This is last month's balance sheet." He pointed toward the screen without looking. "We've accumulated a sizable cash reserve and we're ready to make a few acquisitions."

"These next slides show some of our operations in Singapore and Mainland China." He rapidly clicked through images of factories and offices, some with signs written in both Mandarin and English.

Mr. Jacobsen turned off the projector and laid the remote down on the table. He lowered into a chair before arranging himself, elbows resting and fingers pressed together beneath his chin like a pyramid. Josh resisted the urge to leave the room.

"Well?" Mr. Jacobsen asked.

The other men were now sitting in a similar fashion, all staring at Josh.

"Excuse me?" Josh said.

"Son, I think maybe we're about done." Jacobsen sighed. "I brought you here to show you our operation, complete with a tour of our R&D lab and Engineering Department." The exec arched his eyebrows. "That's all you have to say?"

"I'm not sure what to say," Josh replied. "It's a beautiful facility."

"That's more like it. Your type just doesn't understand how businesses like Magma operate."

Mr. Jacobsen smiled. All the VP's smiled. Jacobsen said, "Maybe it's time to let it go."

"I'm sorry," Josh said, feeling his face tighten. "Let go of what?"

"Owning and operating a business."

Baker's Dozen

"Are you making me an offer?"

Mr. Jacobsen laughed. All the VP's laughed with him.

"Son, I'm offering you a job. You can start in production, just like I did, and in a few years, maybe work your way up to engineering."

Josh leaned back in his chair. "I don't recall applying for a position with your company."

Mr. Jacobsen slapped the table with his hands and stood. All the VP's stood with him. "I've got a busy day, ahead," Jacobsen said. "Take some time. Think about it."

Mr. Jacobsen fished an envelope out of his inside coat pocket and handed it to Josh. "Here's six tickets to next week's game. The Cubs and Sox. Go to the game. Drink some beer. Call HR if you have a change of heart." Mr. Jacobsen abruptly left the room. Two of the VP's abruptly left the room behind him.

Josh opened the envelope and peeked inside.

"I don't know where the tickets came from," said the third VP, Mr. Nordstrom. "Jacobsen doesn't like baseball. By the way, I'm supposed to accompany you on our boat for lunch."

"It's only 10 a.m.," Josh said.

"I know, but Mr. Jacobsen thought you might enjoy an hour on the lake," Nordstrom said, staring at his phone. "It's really nice. You'll like it."

Josh put the tickets in his jacket pocket. "I *am* a little hungry."

"Good, let's head down to the slip."

Nordstrom pressed a button on his phone. "It's a go. We'll be down in two minutes."

Josh followed him into the corridor where they waited for an elevator. The VP stared at his phone until the elevator arrived, reading emails -- then entered without saying a word. Josh stepped inside, standing next to him, riding the elevator down to the lower level.

The doors opened into a small lobby where a man stood waiting. "Good morning, Mr. Nordstrom."

The attendant turned to Josh, his smile flattening into a thin line. He pointed to a safety sign on the wall. "Please read the instructions. Life preservers are located under the seats."

A minute later, the attendant opened a door through which the engines of a Bertram 80 cabin cruiser gurgled. Josh and Nordstrom stepped out onto a concrete platform which surrounded the yacht, moored in a private boat slip. On the wharves, giant concrete columns supported the building above. Two men in striped shirts waved through an open window of the flybridge. "All set," one of the men shouted.

Nordstrom stepped onto the boat, then down onto the rear deck where two women, in their twenties, stood waiting like uniformed flight attendants. Josh followed him.

"Please sit down until we get out into the river," a woman with shoulder length blonde hair said. Josh sat on a cushioned couch surrounding a fixed table on three sides. "May I offer you a drink?" she asked him.

"Do you have orange juice?"

"Sure." Standing at a serving table, she lifted a tumbler then used tongs to drop a few cubes from an ice bucket into a glass. She dispensed orange juice into the tumbler through a bar valve with many buttons, then handed the drink along with a napkin to Josh.

The idea of working for Magma Electronics seemed foreign to him. It wasn't part of his plan, yet, their organization and success intrigued him. He'd received a letter and responded a day earlier. It didn't make sense.

Standing on the pier, the man from the lobby unwound the last of several large ropes from a capstan. He tossed the rope to the ship's mate who'd stepped down from the flybridge onto the walk atop the stern.

The boat backed slowly into the north branch of the Chicago River, coming to rest in the center for a moment before shifting gently forward. The attendants nestled around Mr. Nordstrom who cradled a Bloody Mary in his lap.

The VP lifted a hand and pointed his thumb behind him -- toward the bow. "If you wanna see the interior of the boat, feel free.," he said, now wearing dark sunglasses. "The head's located through the galley toward the front."

Josh stood and tested his sea legs, then walked on the rear deck through a double sliding glass door into a Swedish style galley -- built-in white sofas flanking both sides. He stepped around a long bar, admiring the sleek design, then down a short corridor toward the front of the yacht.

Near the front of the middle deck, presumably under the upper flybridge, he entered a fully functioning office surrounded on three sides by windows through which he admired the Chicago skyline for a moment. Who would find time to work on such a nice boat? he thought as he wiped his fingers along the ebony wood top of a barren desk resting in the center of the minimalist space -- an ergonomic chair tucked under.

Josh stepped around the desk to peek inside a half bath where towels embroidered with the Magma logo hung neatly over a bar near the sink. On the other side of the bathroom, a spiral stairway led down. He ducked beneath a "Watch Your Head" sign, descending to the lower deck.

Downstairs, he waited for his eyes to adjust to dim lights along a corridor. Directly to his right -- toward the bow -- he peered into the master suite at a kingsized bed with red satin covers and lots of pillows arranged neatly on top. Portholes lined both sides of the large room. He turned and wandered slowly down the corridor -- assessing two additional staterooms, each nicely furnished and each with a private head.

On his way back toward the stern, he couldn't help but imagine wild parties on the yacht while anchored miles offshore. It was a life he'd never known. Though reluctant to admit it, the images of excess frightened him. He'd been offered every drug imaginable at parties, sometimes making a joke of his abstinence. He'd once told James, his best friend, "I'm taking the high road." James had overdosed on heroin not long after.

Climbing the rear stairway, Josh noticed vertical, linear patterns in zebra wood bulkheads on which hung framed photos of sunburned executives -- each grinning on deck with their catch -- mostly salmon and trout presumed caught from Lake Michigan. Though his father could have easily provided a life of privilege, Josh had begun his journey from the ground level.

Upstairs in the galley, peering across glistening water through a large window on the port side, Josh recognized the back side of the Chicago Institute of Art and the West Mart Center -- both above a retainer wall -- as the boat approached a bend.

He returned to the rear deck where the threesome relaxed in the midday sun -- eating finger foods, uninterested in his movements.

Josh selected a quarter sandwich and sat -- listening to the water lap the sides as they pushed slowly along the river -- drifting between the most beautiful buildings in the world.

Minutes later, the yacht passed through a lock to open, blue green water -- the Chicago skyline shimmering in opulent defiance to the hardscrabble lives of ordinary people.

CHAPTER EIGHT

Dressed in her faded jeans and smock, Janie shuffled down a concrete stairwell toward voices and the smell of coffee. Across a lower corridor, the midget, Rex, and his partner, Drew, sat at a table in the break room -- both without makeup. "Good morning," she said softly, standing in the doorway with her arms wrapped around herself.

"Have some joe and a donut," Rex growled, pointing at a coffee urn next to an open box of assorted pastries, both on a nearby table.

She pumped coffee into a styrofoam cup then lifted one of the large, chocolate glazed donuts from the box.

"Cream's in the fridge, if you want it," Drew offered.

"No thanks, I take it black." Cream was a luxury she'd long forgotten. She lowered herself onto a bench then bit into the toroidal confection.

Freddie burst through the door from the warehouse, startling Janie. He stepped across to where she sat, hovering only inches away. Her eyes searched the room for relief.

"Don't worry about Freddie," Drew said, fingering his coifed red hair. "He doesn't always respect personal space." Drew shook his head at the young man. "Freddie, pul*lease* don't crowd Miss Janie."

Shifting his gaze to the box on the table, Freddie grabbed two donuts, putting one into the pocket of his blue, Illini sweat pants. White powdered sugar dusted the front of a matching sweatshirt as he bit into the other.

"Does Freddie live here?" Janie asked.

"Yeah," Drew said. "Most of the time. Josh took him in after he turned 22."

"Where's his mother?"

Drew narrowed his eyes and barely shook his head, signaling for her to change the subject.

Janie acknowledged the gesture with a slight nod. "So, where do you go with your food truck?" she asked.

Rex and Drew exchanged glances. Rex said, "Why do'ya wanna know?"

"Just asking." Janie bit her lip.

"Are you a cop?" Rex asked.

"No."

"It's not nice to steal," Freddie said.

"I'm sorry . . . what?" Janie asked.

Drew said, "He repeats phrases sometimes out of the blue. Don't worry about it." Drew cocked his head. "I love your smock top," he cooed. "Did you make it?"

"I got it at the thrift store."

"Oh."

The door creaked. Harvey ducked under the opening -- still wearing his lopsided overalls -- followed by Rosie. The giant man pumped two cups of coffee.

Drew and Rex exchanged glances again. Rex cleared his throat, then said in a raspy voice, "We go to construction sites and around some offices at lunch time. We try to keep a regular schedule, but unfortunately, we have to change from time to time."

"Do the police bother you?" Janie mumbled with a forefinger over her mouth -- cheeks bulging.

"Not too much, but the other food truck owners sometime complain."

Janie sipped her coffee. Peeking over her cup, she said, "Why don't you get a permit?"

"*Ha!*" Harvey bellowed abruptly. "If he wasn't such a *freak*, maybe!"

"Quiet, Sasquatch!" Rex snarled. He leaned back, glaring up at Harvey with difficulty.

Drew whispered to her, "You *know*, girl, I got a few things that might fit you."

Her daddy waved goodbye as she cried in the back seat of her Aunt Irene's car. He stood at the mailbox, increasingly obscured by clouds of dust billowing behind the sedan.

"Did somebody hurt you?" Drew asked.

"W-what?"

"Did someone do something to you?"

They were all staring at her. She sat with her feet up in the chair, arms around her knees, rocking.

"No!" she said. Her eyes darted around the room. "I'm fine!"

"You want, I can talk to my guys," Harvey offered. Rosie punched him in the ribs. He held one hand up in mock terror. "Just sayin'."

"It's okay, really," Janie said. "I'm just a little stressed out right now." Her voice trailed at the end. Just breathe, she told herself. Her heart pounded in her neck as she fought the urge to run outside, away from their probing eyes.

"Why don't you come shopping with Rex and me?" Drew said. "We can go to Marshall Field's."

"Hey, everybody back off!" Rosie blurted in a husky voice. "Give 'er some room, willya?

The muscular woman turned toward Janie. "Honey, just take it easy. You're in good company here. C'mon Harv."

Harvey grabbed four donuts, cradling three against the bib of his overalls with one arm, biting into the fourth as he ducked into the warehouse, following Rosie.

"It's not nice to steal," Freddie said again, now eating the second donut he'd retrieved from his pocket.

Janie sobbed.

"Awwwwww," Drew consoled. "It's okaaaay, sweetie." He lifted a napkin from a stack next to the donut box and handed it to her.

Janie took the napkin and blew her nose. "I'm okay now. I don't like when people yell at each other."

"Harvey's just a big teddy bear," Drew said.

Rex growled, "Part of the witness protection program, if you ask me."

Drew regarded Janie with sympathetic eyes while extending an arm in the direction of Rex, patting something invisible in the air -- motioning.

"Ummmmm . . . a pillow . . . uhhhhh . . . ," Rex guessed.

Drew held a finger in front of his mouth.

"One word . . . rhymes with finger," Rex continued.

Drew sighed and rolled his eyes.

"I need to go to the bathroom," Janie said in a low voice.

"There's one down here," Drew said. "Just down the hall to the left."

"No. I left my things upstairs. I'll go to that one."

Drew said, "No worries."

Janie ran across the corridor, then up the stairwell to Josh's room. She fished two twenty dollar bills out of her pocket, returning them to where she'd found them on the dresser.

CHAPTER NINE

Rex said, "I don't like it."

Harvey scrunched his mouth. "What?"

A radial arm saw whirred, echoing through the cavernous warehouse, then whined as Rosie cut a one by four.

"He doesn't look good," Rex continued.

"He's fine," Harvey said, following Rex to the truck. "He's got a lot on his plate."

Harvey narrowed his eyes. "You guys are all the same."

"What?"

"You guys think on an emotional level," Harvey said. "The rest of us don't see all the drama."

Rex grabbed a bar mounted on the back of the truck with two hands. "I'd say you have the sensitivity of a bull, but I don't wanna insult the bull." He lifted himself high enough to place one foot on a metal rung, then hopped up through an open door at the rear of the van.

The little man clumped inside. Raising a crank handle and turning, Rex operated a small gearbox which squeaked from the inside corner of the space, well above his head. Visible through the glass cover, the nylon Baker Electronics banner rolled up into an elongated metal housing mounted at the top edge of the truck on the outside.

Leaning over the counter from the stepladder, Rex bent a long steel rod around a fixed post on the window frame, released it, then pushed the side up. He positioned the end of the rod into a hole on the side, propping the glass canopy.

Pap! Pap, pap! Rex peeked over the counter, through the open side of the van, toward the shop where Rosie assembled a pallet. *Pap! Pap!*

"Whatcha' fixin'," Harv said from across the counter where he now stood, scanning the inside of the converted munchie truck.

"Fix your own dog. I'm takin' one to Josh."

Josh held his face in his hands at the table.

"Josh?" Rex said, peering through the door of the break room

Josh sat up, his tie loose around his neck and his shirt unbuttoned at the top.

"You okay?" Rex asked, waddling toward the table, cradling a prepared hot dog in a pleated paper tray.

"Yeah, just tryin' to get my head around everything." Josh stood and retrieved a bottle of fruit juice from the fridge.

Rex said, "I made you a Chicago dog."

"Just put it on the table, I'll eat in a few minutes."

The little man put the food on the picnic table then hopped in the air, plopping himself onto the bench. "You ate lunch, didn't you?"

"Well . . . yeah."

Josh sat, then unscrewed the top and sipped his drink.

"How was Magma?" Rex asked.

Josh sighed. "It's nice."

The saw whined from a distance.

"Rosie's making a pallet," Rex said. "That's a good sign."

"One pallet for a shipment to the West Coast and one amp to Texas."

The saw whined again.

Rex forced a smile. "Sounds like more than one pallet to me."

Josh picked at the label of his fruit juice. "I think she's got some other side project going. She's been sawing and stacking wood for days."

Josh sipped his drink, then said. "We're gonna be fine." He rotated the bottle cap in his hand a few times, then screwed it back on the bottle, deep in thought. He glanced at Rex. "It's almost like they know what we're planning."

Rex asked, "The mixer?"

"Yeah. I got the nickel tour. They're rubbing my nose in it."

"What makes you think they know?"

Josh screwed the cap off and sipped, then screwed the cap back on. "Just little things he said."

Rex tilted his head. "Who?"

"Mr. Jacobsen. The CEO."

"You met with the CEO? What else did he say?"

Josh folded his hands around the bottle and bowed his head.

"Josh? What did he say?"

"He wants me to work for them."

"*What*?! You *can't*! We're about to turn the corner!"

"Don't worry."

Rex clasped his fingers on the table and twiddled his stumpy thumbs. "Okay, truth here," he said. "I'm worried. Not about the business, but about you."

Josh sighed.

"Why don't you take a break?" Rex offered. "Go to a movie or something."

Josh smirked, shaking his head gently.

"Okay, go for a swim. Do something besides work."

"I enjoy it, Rex. It's what I like to do. Besides, it's like you said, we're about to turn the corner."

The little man continued twiddling his thumbs.

Josh said, "Have we tested it yet?"

"Hmmmm?" Rex peered up at him. "Oh. Not live. Just a few simulations."

Josh nodded.

Rex said, "There's something else, isn't there?"

Josh nodded.

"The developers?"

"No. Not this time," Josh answered. "It's the city and the state."

"What now?"

Josh rubbed his bearded jawline with the back side of his fingers. "They're leaning on us to clean the place up."

"Fine," Rex said. "We'll pressure wash and give it a fresh coat of paint."

"No. Not just that. We have creosote block flooring. It's gotta be sealed."

The little man scratched his chin. "That's not a problem. What about the city?"

"Permits, Rex. I can't keep up with all the permits." Josh gave him the look.

Rex sighed. Motivated by his friend and employer, he'd unsuccessfully applied many times for a food truck permit. Politics. "Josh, it'll work out." He hopped down and moved toward the door.

"Give the hot dog to Harv. And, don't forget to lower the Baker Electronics banner. You know what happened last time."

"Right."

"Where's Janie?" Josh asked.

"She left a few hours ago."

CHAPTER TEN

Both men wore dark suits and white shirts. Both men had black ties and black fedora hats. Both men wore dark, Ray Ban sunglasses.

The garage door opened and a yellow and green panel truck drove out slowly. It turned and rolled slowly toward the van in which the two men sat. The two watched a midget and a skinny, red haired man staring at them through an open door as the truck passed -- BAKER ELECTRONICS painted in large black letters on a banner along the side.

"There they go."

The shorter man with dark sideburns and a soul patch wrote something on a legal pad. The other man sat motionless at the wheel of their white van. Without looking, the taller man said in a monotone voice, "Nice pen. Where'd you get it?"

"Denny's," the shorter man replied.

CHAPTER ELEVEN

"So, how'd it turn out?" Darius asked Tom, who fiddled with his phone.

"I thank it's gude," Tom said. "I did the final mix last night." He plugged his phone into the small sound system used for vocals inside the garage where they practiced.

Austin sat on his stool, making a few adjustments to his drums, waiting for Tom to cue up the music.

Austin said, "Okay, so let's hear it."

BETTER DAYS
(Track 1)

You step on your own mother
just to get a better view
You only smile when you're laughing,
at other people's bad news
You steal from the poor,
you mooch from the meager
you prey upon us all
and you're overly eager

to be evil
to be ugly
to be a devil

There's a little black cloud
pouring rain within us all
it gathers like a crowd
and like the leaves begins to fall
Its kind of hard to contain it,
but most people can restrain
it may seem strange, but it pertains
to me and you,
you and them,
oh them and us

PRECHORUS

Thrown away
and hung out to dry
The innocent days
seem to slip on by
A castaway
in an endless sky
I have my reasons,
but I don't know why

CHORUS

Baker's Dozen

And if you just believe
you will find,
better ways
And if you just believe
you will find,
better days,
for you and me

If pushing comes to shoving
we'll be shoving one and all
We'll be dropping to our knees
and pleased, just to merely crawl
You'd quickly change your mind
and be changing to unkind
Its a disgrace, but when we're faced with it
we'll see,
who you'll be,
oh mercy me

PRECHORUS

CHORUS

I'm starting to collapse
within the traps upon my mind
I shatter like a vase
and place the pieces that I find
I'm picking you apart

and I'm searching for your heart
It's your intentions that you mention
I just don't see,
it's maybe you,
it's maybe me

CHORUS

Austin leaned back on his drum stool, arms folded. "I think it's good to go."

"Yeah," Darius said.

"Thanks, you awl did grite." Tom said. He wrote something in a notebook opened on a music stand.

Sitting at her piano, Marilyn studied the chart. "So, you're okay with me just playing the syncopated chords in the prechorus and the run in the chorus?"

"Right," Tom said without looking up. "Nice job with the backup vocals, by the wye."

"I really like the lyrics," Marilyn said, nodding at Tom.

"Kind of a downer for me, dude," Darius teased. "Kinda like you."

Austin smiled. "Damn! That's cold!"

Marilyn bit her lip. "I think it's a nice message, Tom," she said.

"Oi'm gude."

"Yeah, we got Miss Positivity to help offset . . . you know . . . Mr. Lennon over there," Darius said.

Austin laughed.

Tom smirked at the John Lennon reference. He didn't mind.

Tom's hair hung down over his face as he finished his notes. He wore a blue, orange and red tie dyed t-shirt, faded jeans and sandals.

"Please," Marilyn said, "don't be mean."

"By the wye," Tom said, "did Lech sye anything to anyone?"

"About the video?" Marilyn asked.

"Yee-uh."

"He said he'd be here," she said, looking around at a collection of garden tools hanging on the walls. "Shouldn't we do this somewhere other than here?"

"It's just for the competition," Tom said. "It doesn't have to be a big production."

Darius began playing the bass line for 'Better Days,' memorizing his part. Austin played along with him. Staring at music on stands wouldn't look good in a video.

Boom! Boom!

Tom held his hands up, motioning for Darius and Austin to stop. They stopped playing.

"Tom!" a muffled voice shouted from inside the house.

"What, mum?!" Tom shouted back.

"Keep it down out thay-uh!"

"O kye!"

Darius did his Buckwheat face, eyes wide and mouth open in an "oh." Austin laughed. Marilyn grimaced as Darius adjusted the volume on his bass.

The exterior door to the garage opened. Janie stepped through followed by Lech holding his camera and a light stand -- his pock marked face framed by dark, close cropped hair and uneven beard.

"I don't have much time, guys," Lech said in a thick, Polish accent.

"Don't tell me you're shooting video of the girls over at the grammar school again?" Darius quipped.

Austin laughed.

"Yes, I like the little ones," Lech said, playing along. He put his camera on a shelf, then adjusted the light stand.

"So, what's going on?" Janie asked no one in particular.

Tom glared at her. "I was gonna ask ya the sime thang."

"Uh, oh," Darius said, looking at Austin. Austin laughed.

Janie folded her arms defiantly. "What business is it of yours?"

Tom inhaled and exhaled loudly, maintaining his composure.

Austin squeaked side to side on his drum stool.

"Did you slape with 'im?" Tom asked.

"No. Nothing happened."

"I've told you, if you nade a plice, ye can sty heeah."

"Yeah right. With you and your mother," Janie huffed as she sat on the concrete floor of the garage, her arms around her knees.

"Ooooooooooo!" Darius made his Buckwheat face at Austin again. Austin laughed.

"I'm siving money roit now," Tom said.

Lech said, "Okay, I'm just about ready, so let's talk for a minute, okay?" He lifted the camera onto his shoulder. "Just play along with the song."

"Wait a minute!" Darius said. "We're synching?"

"Trust me," Lech replied, "it's better that way."

"Dude, that's cheesy."

"You can do it. The sound quality will be much better, trust me. I'll walk around shooting with this camera, and . . . Oh, wait! The other camera!"

"It's a Polish thing, right?"

"Yes," Lech said. "Big, dumb pollack will be right back with the other camera and tripod." He jogged through the door.

"Did you see the warehouse?" Darius asked Janie.

She didn't respond.

"Janie?" he repeated.

"What?"

"Did. You. See. Tha. Warehouse?" Darius said, tilting his head from side to side.

"Yeah, it was kinda creepy. He lives there with two clowns."

"You didn't like his room mates?" Austin asked.

Darius smiled.

"What?" Janie said.

"You called them clowns," Austin said.

Janie's eyes widened. "No, really. They were so creepy, at least, when I first met them. One was a midget and the other one was really tall and thin."

Austin laughed.

She continued. "Then . . . there was a giant, and his wife had an ax." Lech returned through the door with his stationary camera and tripod.

"Janie," Darius said, "have you been experimentin' with mind alterin' drugs again?"

Austin laughed.

"*No*! I swear to *God*! Then, Freddie was lurking in the *shadows*!"

"Okay ya'll. That seals it," Austin said. "I'm definitely going to visit Josh at the warehouse."

"Yeah, me too," Darius said. "He's up to something. Always knew that dude was about to crack."

Lech adjusted the stationary camera on the tripod.

"What was he like at Northwestern?" Marilyn asked.

Darius gave her his smirky attitude face with his eyes angled toward her. "You 'bout to bust out of them britches, woman. You done had us all fooled with that whole June Cleaver thang you got goin' on, now you fixin' ta' jump po' Mista Josh's bones."

Austin laughed.

"He seemed very nice," she said, pattering at the weighted keys of her muted, Yamaha electric piano.

"He seemed very nice," Darius mocked. "Well, actually, he *is* very nice. *Too* nice. He just like *you*. Somethin' *up* with *that* dude."

"That's grite, funny man. I know you blokes are *toit*." Tom said, turning to Marilyn. "They played togetha for yee-uhs."

"We still tight. *C'mon* now. I's just having a little fun with the white girl."

"He don't mean no harm, ma'am," Austin said. "Darius ain't been 'round many folks on the outside . . . you know . . . since he got out."

"Oh, roit," Tom said, rolling his eyes. "Don't let 'im ply that whole sha-ride."

"You know, Thomas, for a minute there," Darius began in a serious tone, "I thought you might allow a decent fellow like myself, a bandmate at that, to engage in a little theater with our radiant, Miss Marilyn."

"Now, that's the Darius I know," Tom said.

Austin laughed.

Darius continued, "But, if you must know, dear lady, our esteemed Joshua Baker is an amazing and multi-talented man. He graduated Magna Cum Laude with dual degrees in electrical engineering and marketing. I can testify as a witness, your grace, that he never once cracked open a book. He CLEP'ed most of his classes, so we played music together. After college, when he wasn't offering consulting services to struggling companies, we still played music together."

Marilyn tilted her head. *"Really?"*

"Absolutely. That dude can turn a company around faster than you can say Smokey Robinson. I dare say, I believe he might be capable of the impossible task that lay before us as we stand."

Tom said, "And what, Mr. White, moit that be?"

"He might. He just might, dear Thomas . . . be able to help *us*."

"I doubt it," Tom responded.

"He's not your enemy, Tom," Austin said.

"Well, he also doesn't walk on water," Tom said. "Besides, what makes ya thank we nade help?"

"Well for starters, we need a place to practice. Your mom's about to cast both you and our equipment out into the wilderness."

CHAPTER TWELVE

Janie poked her head through the open garage door of the warehouse. "Hello?"

Darius brushed past her, walking into the center of the space, looking around. "Man, this place needs some work."

"I know they're here," Janie said, pointing at the van, the Range Rover, and the Harley -- all parked in a row against the opposite wall.

Austin followed Darius, surveying the open space, his hands in his pockets. Janie looked over her shoulder at Tom and motioned for him to follow, then stepped inside to join Austin and Darius.

"Yee-uh, I sae what you were tawkin' 'bout, Darius," Tom said. "Josh is a reg'lar Kang Midas."

Darius shook his head. "You just wait, Schlepstein, *you'll* see."

Austin poked Darius and pointed at the mezzanine. "Can you imagine the *party* you could have in a place like this?" Darius nodded.

"All I sae is a dusty warehouse," Tom said.

"Well, there you *go*." Darius said, still looking around. "Always looking for the positives."

Tom shook his head, finding the space interesting nonetheless. Light filtered through dust covered rollout windows high above their heads, lined together in groups of three at the tops of the painted brick walls all around. An old bridge crane sat frozen in time over the shop area, perched on rails that ran both sides of the space below the windows. The rails were supported by regular columns of brick built into the walls, sectioning the space. Tom was no expert, but he knew that sound would travel well, the inset design of the walls helping to damp the reverberation.

They slowly walked toward the offices, absorbing the spacious area around them. Janie pointed. "That's where Josh lives."

"Thank you, Janie. We would'a never guessed," Darius said.

"Hey!", a man's voice shouted from behind them. They stopped and turned.

"Sweet mother of *Jesus*, what the *hell* is *that*?" Darius said through his teeth, smiling and waving.

Janie said, "That's Harvey."

The giant man walked boldly across, carrying a push broom. He glared at Janie. "Who're these people?"

"We're all friends of Josh," she said.

"Does he know you're comin'?"

Janie scuffed her sandal on the black wooden floor. "Well. No."

Harvey sniffed, seeming to assess the odd assortment of smiles pasted on their faces.

"He's in the auditorium with Rex," Harv said. "I'll show you, but if he's busy, then you gotta go."

Harvey, dressed in jam pants and a t-shirt, led the way, still holding the broom. Janie stepped quickly, trying to keep up with him. Darius glanced at Austin and Tom, his eyes wide in mock terror. Austin smiled.

They entered a door and followed a corridor past a break room converted to a kitchen and a bathroom and employee showers on the other side. They continued to the end, following Harvey who pushed then ducked through a set of double doors into a dimly lit auditorium.

Josh stood under the lights on a stage built into the opposite wall of the two story space. The floor angled down with old wooden seats folded up on cast iron frames. They wandered down one of two aisles separating the folding seats into three groups.

Austin whistled in awe. Darius smiled broadly and waved at Josh who'd turned.

"I found these folks outside," Harvey said. "If you want, I can show them the door."

"Thanks Harv, that won't be necessary."

Josh motioned for the group to join him on the stage. "C'mon up."

They followed Harvey up four steps built into one side of the stage. Faded maroon curtains hung on each side of the space. Tom's eyes widened. Stacks of vintage amplifiers lined the side wall behind the curtain on the opposite wing.

"Hey Rex, come down here with us," Josh shouted.

"Okay," Rex grumbled from the control booth, now visible in the center of the wall through which they'd passed to enter the hall. The two story control room protruded from the wall. Inside the control room window, a man's head moved across, then disappeared through a backlit doorway.

"Good to see you guys again." Josh reassured them with his Kenny Loggins smile. Their eyes travelled along the walls of the space -- absorbing. Josh continued. "Employees once gathered in this area for special events." He turned and walked slowly toward the amplifiers, their collective footsteps echoing through the stage floor.

"We now use the space as a sound lab. Rex and I are testing our latest product."

Josh stopped in front of the amps and faced them. "We have a new line of amplifiers that we think will change the lives of working musicians."

"That's cool," Darius said.

Josh extended his arm to one side, his palm open, presenting his collection of amps. "We used these vintage amps to help us with the design."

Marshall stacks and combos, Fender combos, and Vox combos represented 50 years of music history. Tweeds, blackfaces, AC 30's . . . a guitarist's dream.

Rex mounted the steps and waddled across. "We also have video surveillance, in case any of you are wondering."

"And, this is Rex," Josh said, "the best sound man on the planet."

Janie waved. Rex nodded his large head and wiggled his stubby fingers at her. The outline of a beard matched his thick tuft of wavy dark hair.

"Can you tell us about your design?" Austin asked, still admiring the amps.

"We'd have to kill you," Harvey said.

Josh rolled his eyes. "It's proprietary, but the magic's in the circuitry and software, so it's fine." He used his hand to brush a light coating of dust from a Marshall Plexi head,which rested on a four speaker cabinet.

"The new amp design is fairly standard," he continued, "reproducing sounds that were highly dependent on the dynamics of hard wired components."

"Hunh?" Austin said.

"The old RCA radio designs were amazing," Josh said. "Leo Fender discovered in the 50's that the designs produced rich tonal quality, but it wasn't until years later that everyone realized that it was more luck than genius."

"I've read about it," Tom added.

Josh nodded at Tom. "Yeah, the past few years, a lot of companies jumped on the modeling craze, but most musicians cannot afford the high end equipment."

"Tell me about it," Tom agreed.

"Part of the problem is following the dynamics produced by the circuitry. The old wires and tubes are actually integral to the tone that so many folks came to appreciate. The trouble is, they respond differently at different levels and with changing room conditions."

His short arms folded, Rex scraped a foot against the hollow floor.

Josh said, "That's where we think we've hit on something special." Rex narrowed his eyes, but Josh continued. "We have a fairly inexpensive design that can adjust itself, based on ambient conditions."

"Hunh?" Austin said.

"Our amplifiers use a feedback loop to create a base line," Josh continued. "The tone is still in the hands of the musician, but our amplifier can actually determine how to meet the conditions of the room, even when miked through a sound system."

"I'm not sure what all of that means, but it sounds cool," Austin said.

"Our next project is a mixer board," Josh added.

Rex cleared his throat, now standing, in odd contrast, next to Harvey. "Magma's hot after our design," he said with a rasp.

"I don't think they can respond quickly enough to beat us to the market," Josh countered, glancing at Rex.

"I think I get it," Darius said. "So your mixer design will use your technology to produce the same result, except that it'll adjust the levels for an entire band."

"That's it, pretty much," Josh said.

"You got a patent?" Darius asked.

"Yeah . . . for the amp design," Rex offered, "but we're still working on the application for the mixer."

Darius nodded his head. "Well, I know you guys are busy, so we'll let you get back to your work."

Josh punched him lightly on the arm. "No worries. I'm glad you're here."

Rex groaned.

"You're welcome anytime," Josh said.

"Uhhhhhh," Janie said. "That's kinda why we're here."

Tom glared at her, shaking his head gently.

She continued. "They need a place to practice."

Darius rolled his eyes.

"You can practice here," Josh said.

Darius' eyes widened, now directed at Josh.

Tom squirmed. "You know," he began.

Darius inhaled and exhaled loudly, shifting his gaze to Tom

Tom continued, "We're in tha middle of something roit now. My-be we kin tawk about it and git back."

"I think that's a good idea," Rex added.

"No, seriously." Josh turned to Rex. "They can help us, if they have the time. We need to run some live tests."

Rex sighed.

"Now, that don't sound so bad to me, ya'll," Austin said. "Sounds like we can help each other."

Darius held his breath.

"Way nade ta *fo*cus," Tom said.

"Aw man!" Darius shook his head in disgust. "Tom, you need to open your eyes, dude. This is the real deal."

"Time's tha problem," Tom said. "Between odd jobs and the logistics of gittin' togeth'a, it's had enough jist ta find tha time ta practice, much less travel ta this plice."

Janie sat in the floor, holding her knees, rocking and humming. Josh watched her for a moment. "You can all live here," he said, his eyes still fixed on Janie.

Rex groaned. Harvey coughed loudly.

"Really. We have the space," Josh said. "You can do what you need to do, but you'll all be in one location."

Janie rocked and hummed.

Tom bit his lip. Josh had that look. It freaked Tom out, the way he looked at people sometimes, acting like he cared. A businessman. Tom had fallen for that line before. "Trust us," they'd said. Before he knew it, his original songs were stolen. He had nothing to show for it. Josh's offer sounded too good to be true. Something was wrong.

Josh looked at Tom sympathetically. "Let me give you a little tour. Just think about it. You don't have to answer right away."

Baker's Dozen

"If it's okay, I'm gonna skip the tour," Harvey said.

Rex said, "Me too."

Del Boland

CHAPTER THIRTEEN

Seated on upside down, five gallon buckets, the two men in fedora hats stared at a screen in the rear of the van.

"What're they sayin'?" the short one with sideburns asked.

"Dunno. We need audio."

"Where you wanna go for lunch?" the short one asked, still staring at the screen.

"I made tuna sandwiches."

CHAPTER FOURTEEN

"Watch your heads," Josh warned. They followed him down a narrow flight of steps onto the brick basement floor.

"What's down here?" Janie asked.

Josh said, "Mostly old conveyor parts."

He flipped a switch to a single, bare lightbulb hanging in the center of the room over a table, on which lay a map of downtown Chicago. Portions of the ceiling had collapsed, exposing wires festooned by wire hangers. Conveyor parts were stacked in a heap at one end of the room. Somewhere in the distance, water dripped.

"Not much else to see here. Let's take the freight elevator up to the top level." Josh lifted an expanded metal gate built into the wall and waited for everyone to file into the eight by eight cage. He pulled the gate down and pressed a button. An electric motor whirred above them and the cage creaked, then began to rise inside of a musty brick shaft. They passed a utility area on the first floor but the cage continued, groaning its way until it stopped at the top floor. Josh lifted the gate and led them into a corridor.

"Offices are located all around the mezzanine," Josh said, walking slowly to a door. He opened it and flipped a switch inside an empty office space. "They're all about the same." He pointed down the first corridor. "My room is the third door on the right. This office and my room are both connected to a bathroom. The fourth door on the right is an old conference room converted to a living area.

"Where are the other bathrooms?" Austin asked.

Josh nodded. "Yeah, that's the thing. There's a community wash room with toilets and showers downstairs. They didn't have ladies' rooms back when this building was designed."

He walked down the middle corridor, past more offices on the left until he reached double glass doors in the center of the opposite wall, leading onto the mezzanine. "At one time, the mezzanine was a storage area for parts. All the racks have been removed."

They passed more doors, then turned down the third corridor which completed the U shaped structure surrounding the mezzanine. "These offices are all ten by ten, climate controlled spaces."

At the end of the third corridor, Josh descended a second set of steps. They followed. Downstairs, they could see into the warehouse through a large window.

"Down at the end is where Harvey and Rosie live and work." Josh pointed. "Rosie builds the amp enclosures and covers them with Tolex, adding the grill cloth, then installing the speakers, electronics, handles and feet before packing them into cardboard boxes. She also builds the pallets on which we stack amplifiers for shipping larger orders. "

Josh stepped through an opening into a lower corridor. "There's a few offices down here, once used by maintenance and production people." He opened a double door which led to another space under the mezzanine located directly behind the break room. He turned on several rows of overhead, fluorescent lights. Circuit boards in various stages of completion lay on two large work tables. "This is now our production area. We really don't need all the area out in the warehouse, at least not at the moment."

Josh slid onto a shop stool next to one of the work tables. "This is pretty much the design of our amp." He held up a small circuit board. "It's on an etched circuit board with some small, electronic components soldered in place. This large chip in the center provides logic for our amp design. The mixer's a bit more sophisticated."

Austin and Janie sat on stools across the table from Josh.

"So, where's Marilyn?" Josh asked.

Darius laughed.

"What's so funny?"

"She was just asking the same about you."

Amused, Josh said, "Oh, *really*?"

"Yeah. She don't usually talk that much, but she thinks you're nice."

"What'd you tell her?"

"I told her about all your strange habits, mostly. She ran out of the room and we haven't seen her since."

Josh feigned surprise.

"Naw. She's probably having lunch with her froufrou friends."

Tom said, "I don't thank she *has* many friends."

"Yeah," Darius said, "I think you're right, somethin's eatin' at that one. She's gonna snap and kill a bunch of kids."

Josh narrowed his eyes and tilted his head. "She seemed just fine to me."

"Fine. Now, *there's* a good word. That's usually a word I use to describe the frequent objects of my desire. Like, 'There goes one *fine* woman.'"

"I agree," Austin said, "she's easy on the eyes."

Janie said, "She's just so . . . I'm trying to find the right word."

"Normal," Tom offered.

"Yeah," Janie said, nodding. "*Too* normal. *Too* nice. Nobody's *that* nice."

"I think she has a great voice," Josh said, "and she seems to know her way around the keyboard."

Darius nodded. "Yeah, she got talent."

Josh pursed his lips, deep in thought. "Is she reliable?"

They all nodded.

"Is there something going on in her life right now?" he asked.

Austin, Darius, Janie and Tom searched each other's faces. Janie said, "No. At least, I don't think so."

"Hmmmm," Josh said. "Has anyone talked to her about . . . well . . . her *issues*?"

They didn't say anything. Janie kicked her foot against the stool on which she sat. Austin stiffened his arms, pressing his hands deep into his pockets, staring blankly across the room. Darius glanced around at the parts bins against two walls.

"Mind if I ask you guys about the band?" Josh asked.

"Yeah. Sure. Go ahead," Darius responded.

"Okay," Josh began, "so, as a band, what are you trying to accomplish?"

Tom cleared his throat. "Um. We haven't really tawked much about it, but I thank we wanna record some original songs and build a followin'. We're also trying to compate in the Talent USA competition."

Darius angled his eyes at Tom.

Josh said, "I mean, how do you *see* yourselves? What do you think, or, who do you think you are, as a band?"

"I think we're kinda urban cool," Darius said, "maybe with a little funk and blues tossed in."

Tom grunted and shook his head. "*No*. We're strite up Americana, we just haven't got thare yit."

"Austin?" Josh asked.

"I don't care, but it would be nice to play a little country."

"Country's not even a *genre*!" Tom barked. "It's a kitch-all for record execs to mike as much money as they kin!"

"*Some*body's gotta make money, Tom," Darius said. "I know you're independent, but at some point, you *gotta* trust *some*body."

"Sorry guys," Josh said. "I didn't mean to start a fight." He picked up a soldering gun and pulled the switch. A light came on. He released the switch and the light went off.

Darius looked around at the others, then at Josh. "You should call Marilyn. Ask her out for coffee or something."

"I don't know."

Janie wriggled on her stool. "I think maybe she's not interested in guys."

CHAPTER FIFTEEN

Sun filtered through the leaves onto the dashboard of the Range Rover.

"Thanks Dad." Cell phone in hand, Josh glanced up as a woman in blue and white striped shorts and a white tank top rounded the corner, running in his direction along the sidewalk. "I know," Josh said. "It's my responsibility." The woman passed. "I'm sorry, Dad. I've got to go now. I need to speak to someone. I love you, too. Bye." Josh opened the door and slid the phone into the pocket of his khaki pants.

812 Yardley Drive. It was the address Marilyn had given over the phone. "Go around to the back," she'd said.

Josh walked down the driveway, past the large front porch of the prairie style home. He'd visited Oak Park many times. He loved the houses in the area, especially the craftsmans designed by Frank Lloyd Wright.

A yellow finch flew across his line of sight as he admired the neatly trimmed shrubs in the back yard. He stepped onto a small concrete pad positioned below a small metal awning on a two story garage and knocked on the door.

A metallic sliding sound drew his attention to the window, on the other side of which Marilyn fiddled with something. She opened a deadbolt and pulled the door open with some effort. "Hi. C'mon in."

Inside, Josh was surprised by the brightness and space of the converted studio/loft. Stained glass in rectangular frames hung on the walls, reflecting the angular light shining through the west windows. On one side, stairs led up to the rear loft on which a four poster bed and a chest of drawers reminded him of a converted barn featured in Architectural Digest some years back.

"Can I get you something to drink?" Marilyn flip-flopped across the tile floor to a kitchenette located beneath the loft. She wore modest, thigh length khaki shorts and a t-shirt.

"You have any orange juice?"

"How about cranberry orange?"

"That sounds good."

He turned toward the high front wall and discovered more framed, stained and beveled glass pieces, arranged tastefully. "A hobby?"

"Yes," she called from the kitchen. "Well, I guess I've sold a few pieces. It's more of a passion."

In the opposite corner from where he'd entered, an electric piano sat on a table next to a set of congas, an acoustic guitar on a stand, and a number of smaller percussion instruments neatly hanging from pegs on the wall.

Marilyn returned holding two glasses of cranberry orange. She handed one to him along with a napkin. "Have a seat."

Marilyn curled onto an overstuffed, beige chair, holding her drink with both hands. Josh sat on a Wedgwood blue love seat with a pattern of little embroidered flowers. "I love your place," he said.

"I'm moving."

Josh sipped his drink, hoping she'd offer an explanation.

Birds chittered outside. "I can't afford it," she finally said.

"I'm sorry."

"Yeah, me too." She looked up at the stained tongue and groove cathedral ceiling. "It really does have a certain charm to it."

Josh followed her eyes up and nodded.

"So, you wanted to talk to me," she said.

"Um. Yes. I. Well."

Dimples appeared on both sides of her face and the corners of her full lips turned up slightly. She pushed a loose strand of blond hair over one ear and sipped her drink, her remaining hair tied in a ponytail with a scrunchy.

"I'm sorry." Josh said. "Can I please get up, go back to the door and start over?"

Marilyn smiled at him.

"Actually," Josh continued, "I just wanted to meet you."

"Well. Here we are."

"Yes. So, um . . . what got you into stained glass?"

"I love the windows and doors of these homes. My grandparents lived here when I was a little girl and I would walk to the park with my grandfather." Marilyn sipped her drink, her arctic blue eyes cast down for a moment.

Josh waited.

"Anyway, he'd tell me all about the designs of the houses."

Josh nodded, smiling at their shared interest.

"I especially loved the windows," she said.

"Me, too."

Marilyn tilted her head to peer at him with one open eye. She'd probably heard every pick up line under the sun. Though not his intent, Josh knew that men regularly sought common ground as a possible point of entry. "No, really," he said. "I love Oak Park. I thought about going into architecture at one time, but other interests took priority."

"So, you like Frank Lloyd Wright?"

"Of course. I've been several times to his home and studio down the street. I love his balance between design and the environment."

Marilyn leaned forward slightly, showing interest, urging Josh to continue.

"I know that he also designed lamps and windows, " he said, "many using beveled or stained glass."

She smiled, rolling her head from side to side. "Oh my *God*! I thought you were *kidding*. Let me show you my book!"

She launched herself from the chair toward a bookcase next to the love seat, placing her near empty glass on top. She knelt, sitting on her calves, then pulled out a large book, 'Light Screens : The Leaded Glass of Frank Lloyd Wright.' She hopped up and sat next to Josh on the small couch, their thighs touching. Her hair smelled like fresh flowers. She opened the book across their laps and paged through, describing each design in detail.

"I have a little workshop," she said, bracing one hand on his knee to stand.

Josh followed her to a door in the kitchen area. "It's really the washroom, but I converted it." Josh stepped down behind her onto a concrete floor in the narrow space with a worktable along the exterior wall.

He knit his brows, inspecting shelves above the table where plates of colored glass lay waiting to be cut. "Isn't it dangerous to work in a confined space?"

"Yes. I wear a glazier's apron and safety glasses."

"What about the fumes?"

"Good question." Marilyn lifted two hoses from beneath the worktable. "I designed a close capture system, kinda like the ones used on a hibachi grill." She connected one of the hoses to a long vent at the back and the other hose to a diffuser mounted on the front edge. "It's connected to a blower and vacuum beneath the table. The blower carries the fumes across the top to where they're collected, then passed through a HEPA filter before discharging through the dryer vent."

"Nice."

She attempted to edge around, the softness of her body pressing against him.

"Do you have time to go for a walk?" she asked, her blue eyes shining up at him as she squeezed past.

"Sure."

"I'd like to show you a few of my favorites."

Josh followed her outside, then walked next to her, slowly past the house. Eyes closed, she tilted her face up toward the sun, inhaling deeply.

"Tell me more about your music," Josh asked, admiring the oak trees lining the street in front of them.

"Oh, I played the drums in junior high, then played piano in the jazz band for two years in high school."

"And now?"

She seemed to study the sidewalk for a moment, then turned to him.

"I don't know," she said. "I like playing with the band, but it's really just a way to connect with people."

"Excuse me?"

"I'm in my workshop most of the time. I go to a few shows, but I really can't afford to go out, so I just eat at home most nights."

Josh chuckled.

"What's so funny?"

"I knew a girl in college. She reminded me of you, a little bit. Very pretty. She had offers for lunch and dinner all the time."

"I did that for a while. But, it's kinda like using people, you know?" She thrust her hands into her pockets. "It didn't feel right."

"Didn't you meet some nice guys?"

"Yeah. It's kinda weird, and I don't like to sound big on myself or anything, but being pretty isn't always that great."

"What do you mean?"

"I mean, some guys are completely freaked out about it. They're either too shy to talk to me like a person, or if we go out, they don't like the attention I get."

Josh nodded.

"Anyway, it's hard to explain, but it really gets in the way sometimes."

CHAPTER SIXTEEN

Austin sat behind his drums, feeling the distances, making adjustments. He gave it a kick and a fast roll on the snare . . . *brrrrrrrrRAP!* "Man, did ya'll hear that? It's *tight* in here."

He followed up with a roll around the toms and a kick then launched into a standard shuffle. Darius picked up the beat with rhythmic chord tones, tossing in a few snapped funk notes in the offbeat -- just filling a little space to round out the bass and drum "thang", as he called it. The others milled around, moving their cases behind the curtain, anxious to play in the new space.

Austin and Darius stopped, both making a few last minute adjustments.

"There's donuts and coffee in the break room," Josh hollered through half open double doors.

Buddle lump! "*Sweet!*" Austin yelled back.

"I *told* you this was righteous," Darius added.

Tom didn't say anything. They'd all noticed the keyboard and congas, already set up on the stage.

"Oh, by the way," Josh shouted again from the door, " . . . I hope you don't mind if we collect some data while you practice."

Darius and Austin shook their heads, both watching Tom half kneeling with his guitar in front of his amp. Darius cleared his throat. Tom turned and stared at him, then said, "No, I don't moind," in a low voice before turning back to his amp.

"*Naw! Tom* don't mind!" Darius shouted back. The door squealed as it closed on ancient hinges.

Tom struck a chord and played a few riffs, just to hear the volume respond to the empty hall. He leaned over and adjusted a few knobs on his amp.

The door squealed again. Marilyn walked down the aisle then up on the stage.

"Well, helllllloooooo Missy!" Darius said, chuckling. She curtsied wearing jeans and a tan Sheryl Crow concert tee.

Darius, Tom and Austin exchanged quizzical glances while Marilyn fiddled around with her keyboard amp. She stood, hit some buttons on the Yamaha S80, then played a few chords followed by a honky tonk style riff.

"Why don't we run through 'Can You Imagine?'", Tom said. The others nodded, standing at the ready.

Tom tapped the mike. "Is this thing *on*?!" he shouted.

"Try it now!" Rex's oversized head hollered back through the open window of the control booth.

"*Test, test! Chhhh! Chhhhh! Test*! It's a little squeaky ta mae."

"*Test. Chhhhh*! That's betta."

"You're *wel*come," Rex growled from the booth.

"Thanks Rex!" Austin shouted, smirking at Tom.
"Okay, let's go."

CAN YOU IMAGINE
(Track 2)

Can you imagine a world
where everything is born to be free?
Living a strange life
where everything is
what it's supposed to be,
a utopian scene
Whatever that even means

And so it's sad to say
There may never come a day
That we can live in peace and
love and harmony
all across the seven seas

But sometimes we are our own foes
and so it goes
that we don't even know
What we're made of,
or we're afraid of,
but we perpetuate fear

Maybe when we live in lies,

Baker's Dozen

we never realize
how good it can be
Set me free,
can't you see
that we are in control of you and me?

Now I won't tell you (I won't tell)
How to live (how to live)
And I won't tell you (I won't tell)
How to give (how to give)
And I won't tell you (I won't tell)
what to do (what to do)
All I say (all I say)
Is think it through (think it through)

And I won't tell you (I won't tell)
How to play (How to play)
And I won't tell you (Whoa, whoa, whoa, etc.)
how to pray
or what to say everyday
It's up to you anyway

(Repeat 1st verse)

"Lawd have *mussy*, Miss Marilyn!" Darius said
with a smile, "what on *earth* has gotten into *you*?!"

Austin laughed. "Movin' around, groovin' and
smilin'. And ya'll hittin' those background vocals!"

Austin pointed a drumstick and nodded his approval at Darius.

Darius turned to Tom. "*Yo*, and what about that *guitar* tone. Dude, what is goin' *on* in *here*?"

Tom nodded. "Yee-uh, Josh mide a little tweak."

"Man, that was some smooth overdrive . . . like butter," Darius said. "It was better than that. It was positively *ratty*!"

"Thanks, mate."

"*Nice*," Rex shouted from the booth. "How'd you like the sound?"

"*Dude*! I never played no empty hall that sounded like *that*," Darius shouted up to him. "What did you *do*?"

"Nothin'," Rex said. "It's the new mixer algorithm."

"Man, never knew Algo had so much rhythm!" Austin teased.

"Nice work, band!" a familiar voice with an accent shouted from inside the booth.

"Lech? Izzat *chu*?" Darius hollered.

"Yep!"

"Man, ain't you *missin'* somethin'?"

"What?"

"*Recess*!"

Austin laughed. Marilyn and Tom shook their heads, smiling.

The door squealed. Josh led Freddie, Janie, Harvey, Rosie and Drew down to the front row where they each folded down a seat and plopped.

"Sorry we're late," Josh said. "Thought we'd catch the show."

"It's *practice*," Tom said.

"I know. We won't say anything."

"Lit's run through it agin," Tom said, not wanting to engage in long conversation.

Marilyn began the song again, this time looking at the front row as she played, smiling.

Lech moved around with the camera, filming as they played. Freddie rocked in his seat.

They finished their song to applause. Tom rolled his eyes. "It's practice," he said.

Josh said, "I told you we wouldn't say anything." He laughed.

As musicians, they knew the protocols for band practice. Yet, they were seasoned professionals. They could've played on the Titanic as it sank.

"Sorry for the intrusion," Josh said, standing up. "There's something I'd like to say to everyone."

Darius rested his arms on his bass.

"First of all, thanks for helping out. We really need to collect some data so we can put the finishing touches on our patent application."

A few nodded.

"Secondly, thanks for brightening up the place. It's nice to have folks around."

"What are *we* . . . chopped *liver*?" Harv said to Rosie, loud enough for everyone to hear.

"Anyway, I'm still working out a few details, but I hope everyone can get together again at 7:00 in the conference room."

"Yeah. I ain't doin' anything," Darius said.

Austin said, "No problem."

"And, *finally*," Josh pulled an envelope from his pocket. "I have six tickets for the Cubs and Sox tonight. Anyone wanna go?"

"I'll take those," Harv said, standing and grabbing the tickets.

"I'd like to go, too," Janie said.

"Cubs are gonna lose," Darius said. "You'll just get depressed."

Janie stuck out her tongue at him.

Drew waved his hand in the air. "*Me, me*! Please pick *me*!"

"Sure, Janie," Harv said, ignoring Drew. "You can come along with me and Rosie."

"*Me, me*," Drew hopped, still waving his hand in the air.

"I'd like ta go," Tom said from the stage.

"Pick me, please pick me!" Drew shouted, now standing on one of the seats.

Harv pointed at Tom. "Okay, John Lennon can go."

Tom bowed his head in brief acknowledgement.

"And we should take Freddie," Janie said looking around. "Where is he?"

"I like music," Freddie answered from the stage, standing next to the keyboard.

Harvey rolled his eyes. "Okay, Freddie's in."

"What about me?" Drew whined.

Rosie punched Harv on the arm.

"Okay, fruit loops, you can go, but none of your antics."

"Yay!"

Harv handed two tickets to Janie, one to Drew, then one to Tom, who leaned down from the stage.

The opening piano line to 'Can You Imagine' rang out. Marilyn stood to the side as Freddie played the opening chords and the riff at the same time, note for note.

"*Wow*," Tom said. "Amizin'!"

Freddie stopped, revealing a rare smile. He squirmed as Marilyn hugged him. "I like music," he said.

"Oh my *God*," Janie sobbed. That's so *sweet*!" She wiped her eyes with her finger.

A train moaned in the distance. Janie sniffled.

Josh said, "Don't forget, there's coffee and donuts."

Harvey scratched his stubbled chin with his fingers. "Uhhhh."

"Harv?" Rosie prodded.

"There's still some coffee," Harvey said apologetically.

"You *did*n't!"   Rosie punched him in the stomach and chest.   His head hung low, Harvey arched his eyebrows, unmoved by his assailant.

"I thought everybody already had one," he said.

"Harv," Josh said, "there's two dozen donuts."

Someone snickered.

"Harv, there were two dozen donuts, you *pig*!" Rosie scolded, propelling her body away from Harv's unyielding mass with one last shove.

CHAPTER SEVENTEEN

Along the platform, Janie giggled at Drew's runway model strut, exaggerating the movement of his hips with each step behind Harv who spun around -- but not before Drew had resumed a casual stride. Harv glared at Drew's quizzical face.

"He's doing it again, isn't he?" Harv asked Rosie.

"Let it go, Harvey," Rosie said. "Let's just have a good time." She shot a warning glance at Drew.

They took the stairs from the Green Line to the Red Line at State and Lake, then waited for the next train.

"I love riding the ell trains," Drew drawled. "It's *sooooo* much more fun than Atlanta."

"*Hmph!*"

"It's so nice and cozy, standing in close proximity to everybody," Drew said, amused at Harvey.

"Especially the red line," he continued. "It's like riding the Wild Mouse at the county fair, jostling around, bumping into bodies. You never know *what* you might bump into."

"Do your bumpin' somewhere else, bumpkin boy," Harv grumbled under his breath, staring straight ahead.

Inches from Harv, Drew folded his arms and turned away with his nose in the air.

"You look like two lovers having a quarrel," Janie teased.

Harv exhaled loudly and rolled his eyes, standing near the edge of the platform in his Sox jersey.

Lights from the train appeared at a distance. The train clacked rhythmically along the elevated tracks as it neared, then slowed to a stop.

Clusters of people began boarding the almost empty train cars.

Preparing for departure, dozens of Cubs fans held onto the bars. Harvey arranged himself on the opposite side of Rosie, away from Drew, Tom and Janie who held Freddie's hand. The train lurched forward then moved slowly toward Wrigley Field.

Drew pointed to a pedestrian on the sidewalk below. "*Ooooo*, look at *that* sweetie."

The crowd braced themselves as they approached the sharp turn in the tracks, all except Drew who bumped into Tom and giggled.

"I'm with the *big* guy," Drew announced, a few folks tittering in response.

"If we git separated, jist mate at the sates," Tom said.

Janie nodded. "Right. I'll keep an eye on Freddie."

The train slowed then squealed to a stop at the Addison platform. The crowd pressed through the open doors, the sun shining through cracks in the corrugated roof. Inching along, huddled together, they descended the stairs, one step at a time, waiting on the crowd ahead. Stepping down onto the sidewalk, the group moved among fans and scalpers asking, "Got tickets?". Vendors sold Cubs and Sox merchandise from stands lining one side of the narrow path.

Freddie stopped at a booth and pointed. Tom tugged at his wallet while Janie held Freddie's hand. The others moved toward the front gates, beneath the iconic red sign with 'Wrigley Field, Home of Chicago Cubs' written in large white letters.

Harv, Rosie and Drew entered the gate and walked around to their portal, finding their seats in the first level along the third base line.

"*Wow*!" Drew marveled at the crowd, pointing to the outfield seats where fans wore bathing suits. "It's just like going to the *beach*!"

"Haven't you ever been to a baseball game?" Harv quipped.

"*Lots* of times. Nothing like *this*, though."

"I gotta monkey, I gotta monkey!" Freddie yelled from the steps, closely followed by Janie and Tom. Freddie had wrapped the long arms and legs of a blue monkey around his neck. The grinning monkey peeked from behind Freddie's head -- also grinning.

Janie, wearing a Cubs jersey, sat first, then Tom and Freddie at the end.

"Hey *Janie!*" Harv shouted across Rosie and Drew from his position on the opposite end.

"What?"

"You know what you call a Cubs fan at a World Series game?"

"Happy?"

"No." Harv waited for effect. "*Confused!*"

A few folks booed and some popcorn rained down from above.

"Hey Harvey," Janie responded loudly. "I don't always *talk* to Sox fans, but, when I do, I order *fries!*" Tom smiled.

A few cheers came from behind, along with more popcorn thrown at Harvey who opened his mouth, trying to catch a few.

"Hey, it's a *Sux* fan!" someone yelled.

Harvey stood and pointed to himself. "You want summa *dis*?"

"Sit down Harv," Rosie hollered. "We don't want trouble."

"Yeah, listen to your old *lady*, Jumbo!" a voice called.

Rosie turned and began climbing over the back of her seat, but Harvey lifted under her arms, her sneaker clad feet kicking in the air. He laughed. "Right, we don't want any trouble."

The announcer called the name of the third Cubs batter, followed by applause from the crowd. Harvey fiddled with his phone, trying to get the game through his ear buds. Giving up, he pulled the jack and adjusted the volume, holding the phone near his head.

"*Wow*," Drew mused. "Look at the package on *that* guy."

"He's wearing a cup," Janie offered.

"Thompson waves off a sign, stands, winds and delivers," a voice from Harv's phone called.

"*Crack!*" The ball went up toward left field and over the fence as the crowd cheered. *"It's driven toward deep left . . . it's outta here!"* the voice said. The batter ran slowly around, out of the shadows covering first, enjoying his moment in the sun.

"*Touch*down!" Drew yelled.

Harvey shook his head.

The announcer at the game called the next batter over the public address, confirmed seconds later by the radio guy.

The batter adjusted himself and spat, standing in the batter's box, arms lifted and eyes trained on the pitcher.

"Thompson struggling early. He takes the sign, nods, winds."

"*Crack!*" *"It's a fly ball."* Again the ball sailed toward left, but the fielder caught it at the fence, ending the inning. The Sox players ran off the field and music played over the intercom. Beach balls bounced around in the outfield bleachers as girls danced in bikinis.

"Hey *look!*" Drew said.

Images of random fans appeared on the Jumbotron screen with the letters *KISS CAM* at the bottom. Some folks waved and pointed, surprised at their images on the giant screen. Most complied, puckering for a kiss in front of the fans. A few refused, followed by boos from the crowd.

"I'm gonna sit next to *you*, Harv!" Drew shouted.

"You just stay where you are, Petunia. I got Rosie right *here*."

"Oh *Look!*" Drew said.

Janie and Tom appeared on the screen. The crowd cheered, so Tom leaned over and kissed Janie on the cheek. The crowd booed. She puckered her lips so he gave her a chicken peck. The crowd booed again, but the camera shifted to the next couple.

Harvey leaned over. "You call that a *kiss*?"

Janie sandwiched Tom's cheeks with her open hands. "Like *this*," she said. She attacked his mouth in the same way that a starving woman would eat a melting ice cream cone.

"*Jeez*, you guys. Get a *room!*" Harv said.

Tom finally emerged from the entanglement -- pink, wet and uncharacteristically exuberant. "Hi! Ware's Freddie?" he said.

Drew looked around.   "I thought he was with *you*."

Janie stood. "Freddie?"

The crowd began to cheer.

"Looks like the Cubs have a visitor," the announcer said over the speaker.

"*Look*!"

A smiling Freddie appeared on the giant screen, sitting between players with his monkey still perched around his neck inside the dugout. The players rubbed his head and patted his back to more cheers from the crowd.

CHAPTER EIGHTEEN

Josh leaned over, making an adjustment to Kenny Ray's new amp. He sat on a wooden chair in the center of the stage, a single blue light shining on him from above. His '57 Strat buzzed loudly through a single coil so he switched to the front two pickups. He played a standard lick from his repertoire and the amp responded, ringing out loudly and sustaining on the final note he held. He bent the B string and played another single note, alternating the pressure to produce a BB King sound. One note could say so much, at times. He followed up with a flurry along the A blues pentatonic, another standard riff, but added a few Dorian notes to give it more depth from a jazzier, blues perspective.

He'd taught himself guitar in college. Over the years, his Strat often rested, encased under his bed for months, as he'd focused his energies elsewhere. He'd return to his old friend, always surprised to discover a few new chops in his repertoire.

He'd experienced the same with subjects in school, sometimes going to sleep after studying, then waking up with a solution to a particularly difficult engineering problem.

With his guitar, he'd found a new level of understanding from a place that he couldn't explain -- a spiritual experience.

Josh played another long sustaining note, feeling the sound in his body as the tone from the new amp emulated his prized '65 Fender Deluxe Reverb, now sitting in retirement among his collection with its lovely, aged grill cloth and tattered black Tolex. Josh heard the chords of a familiar song in his mind, playing the notes along with them on the stage. The tone felt right. The dynamics and range of the amp were to his specifications and he could control them, mostly with his hands.

Somewhere, in another time and place, he might have enjoyed regular gigs, sharing in the experience with others. He ended his short solo, shifting to an arpeggio played over a C Maj seventh chord substitution, then back again to the A minor blues pentatonic.

A light round of applause came from the darkness. Josh squinted, shading his eyes with one hand. Several silhouettes walked together down the aisle. Noisily mounting the stage from the side, Marilyn, Darius and Austin stepped into the light.

"Hey guys. What's up?" Josh called to them.

"Dude, that was *nice*," Darius said.

"Indeed," Marilyn added.

"Thanks."

"Thought we'd take a little break," Austin said.

"Break from what?"

"We're moving in, dawg." Darius grinned.

"*Awesome!*" Josh and Marilyn's eyes met briefly before she feigned an interest in her keyboard, pattering the keys -- the notes to which only she could hear, Josh surmised.

Austin positioned himself on his drum throne and gave a double kick which echoed in the surrounding space. "Sounds a little different."

Josh nodded.

Darius strapped on his Fender Precision bass and flipped the switch to his amp. "Shall we?"

Marilyn sought direction with just a look, a subtle communication among gigging musicians. Like many other professions, a common bond tied their specific areas of knowledge and skills together -- a desired outcome through cooperation.

"Missy, just pick it up wherever it feels right. I'd like to run through a few 12 bar blues standards with my ol' friend, Mr. Baker."

Josh caught Marilyn's eye. "A Hammond organ sound usually goes really nice," he said, standing. Marilyn flipped the switch, waited for the electronic display, then made a selection.

"Let's warm up with a moderate tempo swing in G," Darius suggested. He quickly counted two beats, then jumped right into a Freddie King instrumental. Marilyn caught up on the second time around, filling the air with a simulated Leslie rotating speaker sound. Darius and Austin both smiled approval, nodding their heads in time.

Rex appeared down in front of the stage, head tilted, absorbing their impromptu performance resulting from combined physical elements of steel, wood, flesh, neurons and electrons. Josh nodded at Rex, tapping the dead mike on the boom stand between measures. Rex disappeared into the darkness.

Near the end of the song, Austin applied a few standard rolls in preparation for the moment when, watching each other, they hit the last beat in unison.

"*Love* it!" Rex shouted from the booth.

"'Route 66' in A," Darius called out, followed by another quick count.

After the first time through, Josh stepped to the mike, singing the first line.

On the second line, Marilyn sang harmony with him.

"Yeah, *that's* right," Darius yelled.

They all sang the last line together.

CHAPTER NINETEEN

Josh stood at the head of the conference table, now positioned in the center of the room with office chairs neatly spaced around it. Janie noticed the couch and leather chairs had been removed.

Everyone but Harvey and Lech sat at the table. Harvey leaned against the wall near the door, still in his Sox Jersey and jeans, his arms folded in protest after losing to the Cubs. Lech fiddled with the controls on the side of his Sony video camera, standing close to Josh. The filmmaker lifted the camera onto his shoulder and a red light came on above the lens. He panned around the group, some making faces, then he quietly walked around the room.

"Okay, let's get started," Josh said. He touched a button on a projector which whirred to life at his end of the conference table next to a laptop. Icons arranged over a background image of the Milky Way from his computer appeared on the wall behind him.

Janie shushed.

"Thanks for your time. I'll try to keep it short." Josh lifted the cover over a flip chart mounted on an easel behind him, revealing a blank page.

"Some of you are aware of our new technology at Baker Electronics. I'm preparing to roll out a new, virtual mixer board that we demonstrated earlier today."

He leaned down, lifting something from the floor -- a small, blue box with knobs on it -- then set it on the conference table.

"This is a prototype of an interface which will connect to any computer by Firewire or USB. It offers typical hand controls, but it's really only an option. The mixer system is built into the software, supplied as part of a bundle."

Josh clicked his laptop and the image of a virtual mixer board appeared on the screen.

"Or, from any computer, virtual controls may be adjusted on the screen, just like a traditional mixer board."

Josh pointed at a few of the controls projected on the screen with a yardstick.

"But, our design goes a step further. We've created a feedback loop which measures the ambient sound in a room, helping to balance levels to specified settings."

Rex cleared his throat and said, "Just so you'll know, my job as a sound man was to balance the instruments based on the acoustics of any given space. This device helps smaller bands achieve the same results without having a sound man. It's built into the design, so they can focus more on their music."

"We heard the results today," Darius said. "I must say, I'm impressed."

Austin raised his hand. "How does it work?"

"Glad you asked . . . ," Josh began.

Rex cleared his throat again, "but we can't tell you."

"Well," Josh began again, "I *can* tell you that the code is the proprietary part of the design. Most of the remaining design is well established in the industry, but our unique software uses a database of specific parameters that we've collected over the years."

"Parameters?" Harvey said. "That reminds me. When's dinner?"

Austin and Marilyn chuckled.

Rex sighed heavily. "Dinner's downstairs, *after* the meeting."

"*So*," Josh continued, "the software uses input from microphones . . . " Josh paused to fish two, round black objects from his shirt pocket and then held them up, "like these." He laid the two small mikes on the table and continued, "Also part of the bundle. They're placed around a room, providing wireless feedback to the system which quickly finds the right balance, given the surrounding conditions. If the room is full, the sound changes. Our system can change with the conditions. If you're outside and the wind blows, the system changes. The system can also integrate noise cancellation technology to offer the cleanest, most balanced sound possible."

"How much does it cost?" Janie asked.

"Good question. We're offering a complete system including peripherals for around $5,000."

"That sounds expensive," Drew said.

"Not really," Josh replied. "Not when compared to traditional mixer systems. But *wait*, there's *more*."

Austin laughed at the infomercial reference.

"Small bands can license the technology, using only a few peripherals. They can try it on for size and make a later decision to buy the whole package."

"I don't get it," Austin said.

"I can deliver a licensed, software based system online with a code that times out. As long as the code is valid, the system works. When the code expires, the system doesn't work."

"So, what does it cost, say for a band like ours that wants to try it one time?" Darius asked.

"Good question. The wireless mikes are the only necessary peripherals, and they're inexpensive, only a hundred bucks each. They buy the mikes which can be used again and again, then go online for the license. The first time is free. They can check it out and then pay $50 for each subsequent use, or pay for a lifetime license."

"Dang," Austin said. "I'll bet Rex won't set up and work four sets for $50."

"Nope," Rex confirmed.

"The beauty is, they can try it out, use it a few times, or decide to go another direction. They have very little invested, but we receive a revenue stream based on usage in the meantime."

"What?" Austin asked.

"The amp business is typically a one or two shot deal. We build products that are sold, but there's very little income from each customer after the initial purchase. This design provides a regular flow of license fees."

"*Ohhhhhhh*," Austin said, leaning back in his chair, his head supported by his clasped hands.

"Any of this gets out," Harv said, "you go for a swim in concrete boots."

Josh cleared his throat. "I have a proposal." He surveyed the group, checking to make sure he had their attention. "I'd like to offer jobs to those of you who may be interested."

Austin, Darius, Marilyn and Janie smiled. The rest stared in disbelief, not making a sound.

"But, I can only do this with your help," Josh added.

Rosie leaned forward and rested her folded arms on the table. "What does *that* mean?"

"It means that it's only possible through a flex compensation plan."

Rosie groaned.

"Hear 'im out," Rex said.

"I can offer shares of the business as one option. That allows you to invest in the company, sharing in the profits, but also risking some loss of income."

Rosie smirked and shook her head.

"I can offer a place for you to live and meals. You're all free to continue working at your other jobs."

Austin laughed.

Rosie said, "Hey Josh, the only person with a *real* job is professor Tom. The rest of us are making ends meet with odd jobs. The guys with all the money ain't sharing it."

A few laughed.

"Darius?" Josh looked at his old friend.

"Dude, a few of the rungs broke on the corporate ladder I was on. I'm working part time at a shoe store."

"Austin?"

"It ain't no picnic, Josh. Times are tough."

Darius stretched his long arms. "I don't know 'bout all *ya'll*, but *I* think it sounds generous."

"I wanna hear more," Rosie said.

Tom's eyes traveled from Rosie to Josh. "Yee-uh, mae too."

Darius glared at Tom. "Dude, you're like a few years away from tenure at Columbia. What is it to *you*?"

"Hold on a second. Please," Josh continued. "Here's the deal. You're all here because I asked. I know some of you haven't moved in . . . it's your decision. It's here if you want. As for the compensation, those who want their money up front, I'll work something out. I can't pay a lot, but

I'll give you the option to take gain shares, or to accept a straight hourly rate."

"I'll stick with my hourly rate, thank you," Rosie said.

Josh turned and began scribbling with a Sharpie on the flipchart, the paper squeaking in resistance as he wrote.

They waited. He stood and inspected it for a second then returned to write something else. He smacked the marker into a tray and turned to face them, standing to the side so they could all see.

"Here's how the plan works," he began. "You take Option A, and receive 5 shares each pay period as part of your overall compensation. The value of the shares depends on the business, but they will pay a variable dividend, based on each reporting period."

"How much are they worth now, and what is the current dividend?" Rosie asked.

"Good question. I don't know yet. I won't know until the dust settles a bit. If you're interested, you'll just have to trust me."

Rosie groaned.

Tom raised his hand slightly, then spoke. "Josh, I thank ya have gude in*tent*ions, but I gotta sye, my stomach stahts to tighten when I hee-uh execs askin' fokes to trust 'em."

Rosie nodded.

"Fair statement. But, I ask that you think about it. You can go with Option B, which is the hourly rate. Try it on for size, if you want. But here's what I'd like to receive from you in return."

Josh flipped the chart, then wrote again with the marker. After a moment, he moved, allowing them to see his notes.

"As you can see, I've outlined specific duties with some assignments."

Josh sipped a bottle of fruit juice, giving them all a moment to read the chart. He screwed the cap back on and looked around. Placing the bottle on the table, he said, "I understand how you might have some reservations. This enterprise hasn't proven itself. I get that. But, I have a lot at risk here. I've got bills to pay. I have issues to address every day. I'm not exactly living in the lap of luxury. Instead, I'm right here with you. There are no secrets. There's no hidden agenda. It is what it is."

He turned and pointed at the flipchart with his yardstick.

"Darius, I need your help with marketing. In particular, I want you to build awareness for product value and help penetrate a difficult market."

Rosie groaned.

"Harvey, I'd like you to continue helping with facilities and security. A lot of work is needed, so I think it makes sense that we all wear multiple hats."

Rosie groaned again. "I've heard *that* before."

"Rosie, I'm not asking anyone to work around the clock, but we need to work together. I'm not the enemy here."

She nodded reluctantly.

"So, Harvey, I'd like you to assemble a team to help you, at least until we get the place up to code and spruce it up a little."

Josh waited for a nod from Harv before resuming.

"Rex will continue to help me with engineering and assembly, but we'll need more help. Anyone know how to solder?"

Austin and Marilyn raised their hands. Josh pointed at them. "Good, so . . . Austin and Marilyn, I'd like you both to help with production."

Rosie cleared her throat.

"Rosie, you've got enough work on your plate for the moment, but we'll get you some help when we start to ship more product."

Janie raised her hand. Josh nodded at her then reached for his drink, screwing off the cap.

"I can help cook," she said.

Austin and Darius laughed hard.

"What's so funny?" Harvey asked.

"*Girl*?" Darius began. "You remember that time you cooked breakfast for us after that late gig in Shaumburg?" Austin couldn't stop laughing.

"It wasn't *that* bad," Janie sniveled.

"You burnt the *orange* juice!" Darius chortled.

"I was trying to thaw it out on the stove."

"Nobody burns *orange* juice!" Harvey said. A few others at the table laughed along with Darius and Austin who'd turned red in the face, slapping the table with his hand.

"Okay, okay, here's the deal," Josh interrupted. "Rex is the cook. But, Janie will help out. Janie will also help with facilities and various office duties."

"Yeah, Janie and Marilyn get the *light* work," Rosie mumbled.

"Your side projects shouldn't be a problem. Rex and Drew, if you wish, continue the food truck while doing your clown thing. When we need more shipping, we'll create a profit center and pay from our books, which will remain Drew's job. Marilyn, you have your artwork."

"Artwork?" Rosie said.

"You'll *love* it," Josh said.

Rosie groaned.

"Darius, Tom, Austin, and Marilyn, do your band thing while Rex and I collect data. Lech can help Darius with marketing, which might include videos for our products."

"What about Freddie?" Tom asked.

Josh looked at Freddie, who pretended to feed his monkey at the corner of the table. "I'll find work for Freddie."

"Don't follow the ways of the world," Freddie told his monkey

Tom studied Freddie. "I'd loik to work with Freddie too, if that's okye."

Josh nodded slowly. "That's fine."

The group rustled. Janie whispered something to Tom. He nodded. "*Hey*," she said, "I think we need to celebrate."

"Didn't you hear the boss," Rex chided, "there's a lot of work to do."

"Actually, I've been thinking along the same lines as Janie, but we need to do a few things first," Josh said.

The group waited for him to continue. "How about a Halloween party?" he said.

"That's six weeks away," Janie whined.

"Yeah, but I'm thinking we can build awareness for the business at the same time."

Darius chuckled. "Oh, so you're talking *big* party."

Austin laughed.

"Okay boss," Harvey whined. "Can we *eat* now?"

"I've got another commitment, but please feel free . . ." Josh began.

The door flung open. Harvey was gone.

Josh shook his head with a faint smile. "Rex prepared dinner. It's downstairs in the break room. Bon appetit."

CHAPTER TWENTY

Janie, Tom and Freddie followed Rex and Drew down the stairs. Halfway down, Janie glanced up at the others lingering at the top. "I can't believe that he gave us a place to live, *then* offered us all a job," her voice reverberating in the stairwell.

Rex turned his oversized head and glared at her from the bottom of the stairs then waddled through the door.

"Yee-uh, it's a little stroinge," Tom said. "I wonder if he really knows what he's doin'."

They filed into the break room where Harvey stood eating fried chicken at a buffet table. "Put some food on your plate and sit down," Rosie said.

At the front of the line, Rex tiptoed to reach across the table, mounding food on his plate. Standing behind him, Drew said, "You sure eat a lot for a little guy." Janie and Freddie began filling their plates while Tom looked back at the others who'd lined outside the door into the corridor, waiting.

Rex followed Rosie to a smaller table where Harvey was seated, shoveling macaroni and cheese into his mouth.

Janie followed Drew to the smaller picnic table, trying to find a spot where Rex, Harvey and Rosie spaced themselves, making only enough room for Drew to sit. "Go sit at the big table with your *friends*," Harv mumbled through a mouthful of mac and cheese.

Crestfallen, Janie stood for a moment, then moved slowly toward the larger table, followed by Freddie and Tom. She placed her plate down, then sat and peeked under her pixie bangs at the four. Freddie slid next to her on the bench.

"I don't like it," Rosie said.

"Me neither," Harv mumbled again, this time through a mash of green beans -- juice trickling around the stubble at one corner of his mouth.

"*You* don't like it?" Rex barked. "I'm carrying the lion's share of the load around here. Now, we've got *more* mouths to feed."

"Hey *Yo*! We're *standin'* right *here*, dawg," Darius called from the buffet line. Austin laughed.

"We've been workin' our asses off and here *ya'll* come," Drew said.

Lech stood in the corner of the room, still filming.

"*Shut that thing off!*" Harv shouted, spewing an atomized spray of liquid into the air.

Rex glared up at Harv. "Dude. *Really*?"

The red light on the camera turned green, then Lech placed it gently at the opposite end of the longer table. Marilyn remained outside the door, arms folded, eyeing the ceiling tiles where

118

cobwebs hung. "C'mon Marilyn, get something to eat," Lech said, now standing at the end of the line.

"Go ahead, I'll wait," she gestured with her fingers before returning them to safety, nestled in the crook of her arm.

Darius made his way across the room with his plate. "I think Mr. Baker has a plan and he's wanting us all to be a *part* of it," he said.

"Nobody cares what you think, *college* boy!" Harv said from behind a chicken breast.

Darius gave him his psycho killer look, then smiled and sat down.

Rosie pointed her finger. "You gotta lotta nerve, coming in here, getting the cushy *marketing* job."

Darius shook his head. Austin shifted his eyes from Darius to Rosie, then back again at his friend.

Janie began to hum, rocking in her seat.

Marilyn quietly sat down next to Lech at the end of the long table. "You should eat something," he said to her. She waved him off.

Harv shifted his weight and farted loudly. Rosie punched him in the shoulder. He stood and stepped over the picnic bench then wandered to the buffet table, taking the last of the chicken and filling the empty space on his plate with mac and cheese.

Lech shook his head.

"Here Ben," Rex called, clicking his tongue. Something bumped behind the fridge. A pink nose at the end of a long black snout appeared. A 25 pound rat waddled to where Rex held a piece of chicken. The rat sniffed and took the food before waddling back to the space behind the fridge, his long, flesh colored tail snaking behind him, then disappearing.

Marilyn put a hand to her mouth. "Oh my God!"

Rex grinned and Rosie laughed hard. "You won't last a *day*!" she chortled.

The fridge compressor and fluorescent lights hummed a dissonant chorus to the clattering rhythm of tableware.

Rex whispered something to Drew and Rosie. The three stood, then walked toward the door where Harv, having discarded his empty plate in a bus pan, met them. Grinning, Rex held the door. "Nighty night," he sang.

Harv said, "Tonight, you may wanna sleep with your backs to the wall," then ducked under, followed by his friends.

"Ya know," Tom began, "slape's tha only escape I git from an overwhelming population of control frakes."

"You got *that* right," Darius agreed. "I don't mind sayin', Rosie the riveter really gives me the wooly boogers."

CHAPTER TWENTY ONE

"Something's up, Gene."

"Yeah. Your pants legs are up, Francis."

The taller man inspected the bottoms of his legs, one at a time, his black pants extending beyond the cuffs of white coveralls. Both men wore black fedoras and Ray Bans.

"Where'd ya get the suits?" Francis said.

"Standard issue," Gene said, "one size fits all." He lifted his black patent leather shoes, one at a time, his coveralls rolled up to his ankles.

"You think they suspect something?"

"Don't worry, we're in disguise. Besides, we're way up here." Gene pointed down at the ground from the expanded metal platform of a jig lift on which they both stood.

"Whaddya think's goin' on down there?" Francis said, resting a pressure washer wand atop the safety rail which encircled them.

"They're planning something big." Gene nodded at the blonde wearing a glazier's apron and safety glasses near the far corner of the building.

"I heard the big one talkin' 'bout killin' somebody," Francis said.

Del Boland

"That's not good."

Two clowns exited the break room, walking across the space toward a panel truck, followed by a black man dancing with a blue monkey.

CHAPTER TWENTY TWO

SIX WEEKS LATER

Austin hauled his bass drum across the mezzanine. "The place is lookin' good," he said.

"Yeah, dawg," Darius said, admiring the exposed red brick walls and clean windows. "Amazin' what happens when folks work together."

"How many you think'll show?"

"Dunno. But I don't think we gotta worry about having enough space for 'em."

Tom sidestepped onto the platform through the door, carrying his amp and pedalboard. Austin motioned with his head. "Have you talked to him?"

"I'll hit 'im up now."

Tom carried his equipment to an area near the front of the mezzanine where Austin resumed his work, arranging his bass drum on a piece of indoor/outdoor carpet.

"*Yo, Tom.* My *friend*," Darius said.

Without looking, Tom said, "Whadd'ya want, Darius?"

"You know how you got this Americana thang goin' on in your head?"

"So?"

"So . . . what if we had somebody to play mandolin or banjo or accordion on a few songs?"

Tom set the amp and pedalboard down on the deck, in front of the bass drum. "Ya got someone in moind?"

"How 'bout Josh?"

"Josh doesn't ply mandolin or banjo."

"Yeah, maybe now." Darius lifted his Fender P bass out of its case and put it on a stand. "You have no idea. That dude can do anything he puts his mind to. He's amazin', I'm tellin' ya."

Tom said, "He's too busy with tha business."

"*Naw*, man," Darius continued. "He needs an outlet. We can help him."

Tom leaned and peered down over the railing at the floor of the warehouse where Josh rolled a cabinet with a double sink out from the break room. "It *would* be noice to expand our range of style."

"He can also help with guitar parts," Austin added, clamping his pedal to the bass drum.

"Yee-uh," Tom nodded, "I admit, he really added a lot at practice the past few wakes."

Tom glanced again over the edge of the mezzanine. "What's he doin'?" he asked.

Darius shrugged and said, "Don't ask me." He shifted his attention to the open garage door where three men stood holding instrument cases. "Look who da *cat* done drug in!" Darius said. "*Yo! Craig!* Up *here!*"

Craig Christiansen carried his trumpet case alongside two other members of the 'Westchester

Horns'. He bounded up the steps ahead of the other two men who took stock of the surroundings.

"Whatcha usin' for a sound system?" Craig asked, eyeing a large projection screen leaning against the office building near parts of a lighting truss on the floor.

"It's comin'," Darius replied. He and Craig exchanged some tricked out, stepwise version of a handshake which ended with their two hands in a cobra position, moving away from each other, fingers flailing. "It's gonna blow your socks off." Darius pointed down at Josh, now connecting braided hoses to stainless drums mounted high on a cart. "That cat got it goin' on."

Harv called from across the platform through open double doors, "Somebody *help* me!" He'd pushed one of the large subwoofer cabinets on a dolly from the auditorium to the lift. One caster was now caught on the metal threshold. Austin crossed the mezzanine to assist.

Craig's sax and trombone players sauntered over, holding their cases.

"Who's the *babe*?" Craig asked.

Darius followed the direction of Craig's gaze where Marilyn leaned from a step ladder in jeans and t-shirt, attaching orange and black garland around the open garage door.

"That's Missy Marilyn. I think the boss may have his eyes on her."

"Oh. Thanks for the heads up."

"Ya'll can put your stuff down," Darius said. "Nobody gonna mess with it. There's snacks in the green room downstairs."

The three men headed to the steps as the subwoofer laden dolly squeaked across the platform, pushed from behind by Harv with Austin guiding. "We have a *green* room?" Austin asked.

Darius said, "The break room."

The halogens dimmed. In a beam of white light, Josh stood near the edge of the mezzanine holding a mike stand. Behind him, a glowing video screen reflected a giant image of his zombie torso.

"Thank you for coming out tonight. We've got a real treat for you," Josh said to several hundred early arrivals scattered among decorated tables on the newly cleaned and sealed floor of the warehouse.

"The band's here," Josh said, pointing directly behind at a silhouette of Austin's drums on a riser in front of the screen. Gauging the tepid response from the crowd by a smattering of applause and murmuring, Josh removed a fake, zombie ear and held it high. "Oh no!" he shouted, feigning surprise. "What have I *done*?" Josh shifted his gaze from the rubber ear in his hand to the crowd, then back again at the ear. "I'm losing my *hearing*," he said. A few folks in the crowd laughed. He put the prop back over his ear then carefully adjusted a fake gash across his forehead.

"As part of your party package, there's red and white wine in front of our reception area," Josh continued.

"We have a reception area?" Austin asked, standing to the side.

"The break room," Darius said.

"Tonight we have The Fallo Wing featuring The Westchester Horns!" The crowd responded with light applause. "Also, we'd like to acknowledge Baker Electronics for use of the space and the equipment. The show starts in five minutes," Josh said, emulating Michael Buffer, the ringside announcer, "so let's get ready to rummmmmblllle!" The opening horns to 'Thriller' blared through the sound system.

Brrrraaapppppp! ding, ding, ding, ding! The *chorus to 'Thriller;* pulsed from inside.

"What're they doin'?" Gene peeked through the open garage door.

Francis watched two alien girls wander past him, toward the end of a short line at the door. "Looks like a party," he replied.

The green alien turned and said, "Look!", pointing at them. "It's Jake and *El*wood!"

"Jake and Elwood! *Cos*mic!", the blue girl replied, antennae bobbing on her head. The aliens presented tickets to Harvey standing at the opening of a crimson rope barrier, wearing half strapped overalls, a soiled, old hockey mask, and holding a running chain saw with no chain.

Brrrraaappppp! ding, ding, ding, ding! Brapppppp! Harvey turned his attention to Gene and Francis. "Tickets please!" *Brrrraaaapppppp! ding, ding, ding, ding!*

Gene looked at Francis who fished a wallet from his black jacket.

"No tickets!" *Braaaapppppppp!! ding, ding, ding, ding!* "That'll be $60."

"For *two*?"

"Each."

Francis handed him six twenties as the alien girls huddled inside the ropes, waiting.

"Wait a minute, you two," the blue alien girl said as the two men stepped through the rope barrier. "Your costumes aren't complete." She searched her alien bag for a moment, then produced a black marker. She grabbed Gene's hand and wrote J-A-K-E across his knuckles. Then, she grabbed Francis' right hand and wrote E-L-W-O then O-D on his left hand. Gene and Francis looked at their knuckles, then at each other, shrugging.

The overhead halogens dimmed from a faint glow to black as the stage lights turned crimson red. A deep drone of a bass note swelled as fog rolled across the mezzanine then down over the front of the reception area where zombies and vampires mingled. Count Blackula emerged from the fog with his bass, playing through a wireless. He walked to the front of the mezzanine then up wooden steps to a short platform diddling an open E note. The windows shook as a spotlight shone on him -- his large projected face on the screen behind, grimacing vampire teeth at the crowd below. He turned and leapt high with his bass from the platform, his crimson lined, black cape fluttering behind, landing on the upper deck as multi-colored stage lights flashed simultaneously with the band's opening chord, revealing the band standing across the stage from left to right; Marilyn dressed as Marilyn Monroe behind her piano in the fog, a small fan at her feet billowing her white dress, Tom dressed in an army jacket as John Lennon on guitar, Austin dressed as a cowboy on drums, The Westchester Horns together near zombie Josh on guitar, followed by Count Blackula on bass.

Downstairs, Janie with her face painted white, poured red wine into plastic goblets from a sink faucet, her Audrey Hepburn neck accentuated by a black and white striped mime shirt. Super Mario and Shrek sang 'Sweet Home Chicago' along with the band, accepting glasses of wine from Freddie the pirate at the front of a serving line. Rosie the riveter sold cd's and t-shirts at a table near the break room. Scattered on her table between Baker Electronics displays, she offered free gifts imprinted with their logo to mostly local musicians and music store employees.

The band ended their opening number.

"Ladies and gentlemen, thanks again for coming out. I'm Josh Baker. This is The Fallo Wing," he said, presenting with his hand. "Be sure to catch them on Talent USA."

Someone shouted, "Woo hoo!"

Josh continued. "I'd also like to introduce The Westchester Horns, folks." Craig and his guys took a bow from their position next to Austin.

"Josh!" Count Blackula called to him, pointing down at the crowd. "Call them up! It'll be fun!"

Zombie Josh turned then nodded. "Folks, we have some special guests here with us tonight." He motioned at Drew with the spotlight, then pointed. "Jake and Elwood *Blues*, ladies and gentlemen!"

Drew searched among the revelers with the light, finding Gene and Francis near the bottom of the stairs. The crowd responded as the band began playing 'Peter Gunn.'

"C'mon up!" Josh shouted over the mike. The crowd urged the two men to climb the stairs, cheering as they acquiesced.

The horns blaring, Jake and Elwood reached the top of the stairs, the spotlight following them. With serious expressions, they both stood shoulder to shoulder, facing the crowd, arms folded.

Baker's Dozen

As the band played, Josh rummaged in a stage bag, pulling out two microphones. He handed them to Gene and Francis. "Just keep the mikes in front of your face and pretend to sing," he told them. "Nobody will notice."

Nearing the end of the song, Josh walked around with his guitar, instructing the band. "'She Caught the Katy' in A." Each nodded.

They finished Peter Gunn in traditional fashion, simultaneously hitting the B chord four times and ending on the E, Craig going high on trumpet.

Josh started the backbeat guitar to 'She Caught the Katy,' then sang along with Tom as Gene and Francis lip synched to the delight of the crowd.

"So, you come here often?" a ballerina asked Harvey at the door.

Someone poked at her from behind. She turned. "No, down here!" Rex shouted.

"Whoa!" She held her hand to her throat. "You startled me!"

Rex grinned in contrast to his sad clown face. "Better lay off Jason. You should see the missus."

Brrraaaapppppp! Ding, Ding, Ding, Ding!

"Jake and Elwood, ladies and gentlemen!" Josh said, his arm extended toward Gene and Francis as they descended the stairs.

"What was *that* about?" Gene asked.

Francis shrugged. "Dunno. I'm going for some wine."

Over the PA, Josh said, "We'd like to play a few originals for you."

PICTURE YOURSELF
(Track 6)

PURE INSANITY
(Track 9)

"We're gonna take a little break," Josh said. "We'll be right back." An obscure Tom Waits song began to play, part of an eclectic mix chosen for each intermission.

"Man, those two have been hanging around for weeks," Darius said to Josh who wiped the strings of his Strat with a towel. "Wonder what they're up to?"

"I don't know," Josh answered. "They seem harmless."

CHAPTER TWENTY THREE

"Gene."

He snorted.

"Gene. Wake up."

They both sat, leaning against the brick interior wall of the warehouse, still wearing fedora hats and shades. Gene instinctively lifted his hand, sipping the last of his red wine while absorbing the scene before him -- the floor littered with party favors and plastic goblets. Fifty feet away, a few weary zombies, dead musicians, and cartoon characters sat in a circle on the floor.

"What happened?" Gene said.

"Dunno. It's all kinda fuzzy."

A voice came from above. "Dude."

"Is that *you*, God?" Francis said. "I've been meaning to chat with you."

"No dude, up *here*."

Gene and Francis looked up at Harvey, standing over them, his mask on top of his head.

"Uh, yes, how can we help you?" Francis asked.

"Wondering, well, if you're not *doin'* anything," Harvey glanced around. "You know, if you don't *mind.* Can you go pick up six or seven dozen donuts?"

Gene looked at Francis. Francis shrugged.

"Sure." Francis said.

"Thanks."

Harvey meandered toward the center of the warehouse, carefully stepping around a naughty nurse sprawled inside of a chalk outline someone had drawn around her on the floor.

"What was *that* about?" Gene asked.

"I think God wants us to feed the multitudes."

CHAPTER TWENTY FOUR

Josh stared at his computer monitor. "Our Google ratings aren't so great."

"I need more content," Darius said from across the desk, seated in a chair. "It takes time."

"I know." Josh clicked his mouse and the printer on his desk whirred. "Lech wants us to see the videos," he said.

"The videos will give us a boost, but we also need articles and reviews pointing to our site."

Retrieving a check from the printer, Josh nodded then scribbled his signature.

"So, how's the cash flow?" Darius asked, examining his fingernails.

"Looking much better. I think we're gonna have a good month."

Lech poked his head through the door. "You guys ready now?"

Josh and Darius both stood then followed Lech down the corridor to the auditorium -- joining the rest of the group who'd begun throwing popcorn at each other from several rows of seats near the front. On the stage, the video screen stood tall behind a cozy arrangement of furniture on oriental rugs, including the couch, end tables, lamps and chairs from the conference room. The auditorium had become their living area -- a place to gather after hours.

"Okay," Rex spoke through a mike he'd installed in the booth, "it's showtime."

The overhead lights went out and the projector displayed a grainy countdown of encircled numbers.

"Is that necessary?" Darius asked.

"Just having a little fun," Lech responded.

On the screen, a shadowy image of Marilyn smiled and waved on the beach, backlit by the morning sun over Lake Michigan.

"Boooooo!" Rosie shouted playfully.

"What's *this*?" Drew's voice drawled from the back. "Where's the music videos?"

"Just a few clips I mashed together," Lech responded from his seat.

The beach scene faded to Harvey and Rosie seated on a workbench in the shop. They embraced and kissed for the camera. "Hey, get a *room*," Lech's voice said from off camera.

The band relaxed onstage in a new scene -- Darius, Austin, and Marilyn sitting on the furniture after a rehearsal, looking at song sheets.

To the side, Janie sat next to Tom on his amp. The camera zooming in, she smiled and waved. "Okay, Miss America," Lech's voice said to her, "what's *your* wish for a better world?" Janie put a finger under her bottom lip and tilted her head.

"*Hmmmmm.* I wish people could live and work together and . . . no more hunger."

Rosie groaned in the audience, "Oh, pull*lleaassse!*"

"*Yay!*" Drew sang from the back.

"*Aw!*" Darius teased, "she wants world peace and no hunger. Where on *earth* did you come up with *that*?"

On screen, Drew stood tall in his blue leotards and pink tutu next to Rex in front of the food truck, both in make up. They poked at each other then launched into a routine, slapping at each other like children, then snapped back to attention like soldiers with their clown feet splayed. The group laughed.

A scene from outside the warehouse appeared. Gene and Francis sat in their white van on a cloudy day -- leaves blowing down the street as the camera moved toward them. Francis smiled and waved at the camera then Gene took off his fedora and hit Francis with it. The audience laughed. Lech's hand appeared from off camera, handing them a cardboard cup holder with two coffees. Francis took the coffees and waved again.

"We should've invited 'em in for the show," Darius said from the back.

"They *can't*." Drew said, "They're on top secret as*sign*ment!"

An image of Freddie appeared. He held the monkey next to his face, both mugging for the camera.

"There's Freddie!" Marilyn said.

"*Awwww*! That's so *sweet*!" Janie said, rubbing Freddie's arm.

"Monkey *look*!," Freddie said.

Marilyn turned in her seat and smiled at Janie and Freddie sitting directly behind her.

On screen, Lech turned the camera on himself, standing inside the empty auditorium. "Okay boys and girls. The moment you've been waiting for. Voi*la*!" He waved an arm, then angled the camera away from his face, toward a blank screen, now appearing as a screen inside a screen.

The song 'Picture Yourself' began to play, the title appearing in large letters on the video followed by Tom singing along with the bass riff.

Can you see yourself from the outside?
See yourself as someone else?
Every once in a while now
I find it makes it easier to be myself

Blurry halloween characters appeared then alternated with images of the band playing on the mezzanine at the Halloween party.

Picture yourself as a politician,
decisions come at a price
Picture yourself as the bad guy,
you'll know why he finds it hard to be nice

Baker's Dozen

Austin appeared on the video in a suit, standing at a podium, pretending to take questions.

The chorus began to play.

Don't know why
no one thinks they're wrong
In some way
we can get along
Even when we just can't relate
Don't know when people learn to hate

At the chorus, Janie appeared on the screen, crying and shouting, shaking her fist in the air. Then, Janie on the floor, rocking with her arms around her knees.

Picture yourself on the street
Don't even know what you're gonna eat
Picture yourself starting trash can fires
at night when you need a little heat

Members of the band milled around in an alley on a cloudy day. Homeless guys stood around a trash can fire in Chicago.

The chorus played again.

Del Boland

Don't know why
no one thinks they're wrong
In some way
we can get along
Even when we just can't relate
Don't know when people learn to hate

More blurry Halloween images appeared followed by Rex and Drew, dressed in their clown outfits, yelling at each other.   In the next scene, they hugged -- Rex wrapping his stumpy arms around Drew's lower thighs as Drew bent at the waist, over Rex's head.

Picture yourself as the rich guy,
a victorious capitalist
Picture yourself as the guy
who didn't try and opportunities he missed

An image of Josh appeared in his office, working.   Then a street scene of Marilyn from behind, running in slow motion down a sidewalk in Chinatown, turning to look at the camera while seductively smiling then pushing her wavy blond hair over her head.

Don't know why
no one thinks they're wrong
In some way
we can get along

Baker's Dozen

Even when we just can't relate
Don't know when people learn to hate

At the end of the video, the wind blows a newspaper page along the pavement as a man lay curled on stained asphalt wearing tattered clothes in an alley.

The audience clapped at the end of the first music video.

On the screen, the title of the next song, 'Pure Insanity,' appeared in a horror style font.

The song began to accompany fast forward footage of traffic from the median on Michigan Avenue -- cars surging forward, stopping, turning.

Take it leave it,
it don't matter it's all the same
Ain't no time or patience
to be playing your game

You're talking about she and me
Its pure insanity
And you choose to hide
well you can stay on your side
but as you turn away
you'll find you're faced with it everyday

During the chorus, Darius appeared in his funkmaster pose, playing his bass in the median at normal speed with the fast forward cars in the background. Images of each member of the band playing the song in the median flashed in rapid succession.

> I'm so tired
> of taking the high road,
> trying to be the bigger man
> In my mind
> I know what's right
> so it's me helps to understand

Janie and Tom stood back to back near a brick wall, their arms folded, both looking straight ahead with pouty faces.

> With so,
> so many people out there's
> no way to see
> eye to eye to eye
> Yeah so I try
> to let it slip away

The scenes changed to a rapid succession of band members playing.

> You're talking about she and me
> Its pure insanity
> And you choose to hide

well you can stay on your side
but as you turn away
you'll find you're faced with it everyday

Again, an image of Darius appeared in his funkmaster pose, playing his bass in the median at normal speed with the fast forward cars in the background. Again, images of each member of the band played in the median, flashing in rapid succession.

Fast traffic continued during the guitar solo.

The video ended with another rapid succession of band members playing.

The group applauded. "Wooooooo! Wooooo hooooooo!" Rosie yelled.

Peeking through the center of colorful concentric circles, Lech held a carrot. "That's all folks!"

The screen turned white. "Lights," Josh said. The lights came on.

Josh turned in his seat. "Lech, did you get a waiver for everyone who appeared in the videos?"

"Yes sir."

Josh poked Darius. "What do *you* think?"

Darius nodded. "I think they're good to go."

CHAPTER TWENTY FIVE

"I know, Dad."

Josh swiveled from side to side in his office chair, fiddling with a remote.

"Right . . . sustainable."

A flat screen television came on. Josh flipped to CNBC with the sound all the way down, but turned back toward his desk, listening.

"Absolutely. Right."

Darius jogged around the corner of Josh's open door to the front of his desk. Josh held a finger to his lips. Darius leaned down into Josh's view, his eyebrows raised, then lifted the remote and changed over to WGN, pointing at the television.

Onscreen, an aerial image of a food truck travelled on Clark Street, followed by three Chicago police cruisers. Josh's eyes widened.

Darius folded one arm across his stomach, holding the elbow of the other arm, studying the live scene.

"Dad. I'm sorry. I gotta go. I love you, too. Bye."

Josh leaned back in the chair and watched. Darius turned up the volume. The food truck weaved slowly from side to side preventing the cruisers from passing. It wheeled around a corner, slowed, then weaved through heavy traffic crossing Washington at midday. One cruiser followed cautiously from a distance, stopping once in the intersection for a taxi, losing ground. The food truck went to the next intersection then edged around the corner against traffic, which slowed at the oncoming vehicle, but started to move again, blocking the way for an ensuing cruiser. The truck darted into a parking garage, out of view.

"This ain't good," Darius said.

"Nope."

They watched continuous aerial coverage of the garage.

A lady news anchor broke in. *"Folks, we're watching what appears to be a slow speed chase through the city. A food truck eluded police but is now inside this parking garage . . . where is it . . . ?"* the anchor's voice trailed. A few seconds later, the anchor continued. "As soon as I confirm the location, I'll give it to you, but Chicago police are asking folks to stay away from the area."

"Hunh?" Darius said. "Now, if they want us to stay away from the area, then why are they wantin' to tell everybody where it is?"

Josh rolled his eyes, holding his phone at his chin.

At the top right of the screen a green and yellow panel truck exited the garage on another street. The camera followed the van for a moment.

"*There appears to be a truck exiting the parking garage,*" the voice on television said.

Josh selected a number from his contact list then held the phone to his ear.

"Rex?" he said. "Hi. Where are you right now?"

Josh nodded. "Ummm hmmmm. Right. Yes, it *is* a lovely day," Josh responded. "So, what's goin' on?" Josh closed his eyes and sighed. "Uhh, Rex. I can . . . Rex. *Rex*! I can see the whole thing on television. What's *that*? You're breaking up." Josh shook his head, then rested his hand holding the phone on the desk. "Unbelievable," he said to Darius. "He's all casual. I heard Drew screeching in the background."

"Yeah, he's a piece of work. You know they'll run the tag number," Darius surmised. "They'll be here."

"Wellllllll . . . " Josh said.

"Well, *what*?"

"Rex has it rigged. He can flip it from inside the cab."

"He's got a phony tag?"

"Yeah. On one side. But the other side's legit."

"You mean, he rides around in a food truck with a phony *li*cense plate?"

"Well," Josh contorted his mouth into an exaggerated grimace, "yeah, kinda."

"*Dawg*! I'm startin' to *like* that clown."

"Seriously?"

146

"Yeah.   For a *little* dude, he's got some enormous reproductive glands."

"Right." Josh rolled his phone in his hands like a bar of soap.

Darius wrinkled his lower lip and tilted his head. "What's wrong? Everything's gonna be okay."

"It's my dad," Josh said

"Something wrong with your dad?"

"Well. No."

"Then what *is* it?" Darius asked.

"He won't be happy."

"Josh, surely you're not gonna *tell* 'im."

"He'll know."

CHAPTER TWENTY SIX

"Man." Josh held his guitar case, staring up at the marquis of the Chicago Theater.

TONIGHT: TALENT USA

A loose strand of Marilyn's hair whipped around her face. She tried using her mitten fingers to tuck the hair behind her ear with little success. Leaning against Josh in his navy P coat for warmth, she admired the great Chicago landmark from the sidewalk.

Darius scrunched his neck down into a black knitted scarf, a dark gray, Irish flat cap turned backwards on his head. "You know what bugs me?" he asked.

"No, *what*?" Austin answered.

"Why come they don't sell green bean juice in cans? It's healthy. It *tastes* great. Why can't they sell it like *vegetable* juice?" Darius braced against a gust of wind, holding his guitar case.

"I don't know," Austin said without looking at him. "Why don't *you* do it?"

"Cause I don't have the capital or the connections. You can't just put juice in a *can* and *sell* it. You gotta bribe a whole bunch of politicians with a cut. You gotta find somebody on the inside at the FDA. You gotta lie and cheat and steal. It's a racket that's far beyond the resources of a humble, *black*-assed, *bass* player."

"You've got a point."

A doorman checked their passes then held the door open as they entered.

"I *love* this place!" Marilyn said.

Josh's eyes followed the opulent second floor colonnade rising up to a vaulted ceiling inside the grand lobby. Ahead of them, a red carpeted stairway arched from two sides, connecting at the second level.

"Wow," Marilyn said. "Neo Baroque, French revival."

"What'd she say?" Austin asked.

"She likes the design," Josh replied.

They continued through the lobby then past the doors leading to the lower level of the dimly lit theater. They sauntered down the aisle, absorbing the great hall. "They don't build theaters like this anymore," Josh said.

"I don't think anybody can afford the skilled labor, or even find the skilled labor, for that matter," Darius agreed, peering up at the arched facade surrounding the front of the stage.

Turning around, Austin marveled at the empty seats. "Can you imagine this place full of people?" he asked.

"Man, don't go gettin' *stage* fright," Darius said. "You been doin' this too long. Besides, we won't see a thing with the lights. Just stay in your zone."

"Right. *Snake! Sssssssssss!*" Austin nipped at the back of Darius' thigh with his fingers.

Darius jumped and spun 180 degrees. "Man, how many times have I done *tolt* you not to do that to a brotha?"

"Ladies and gentlemen, let's give young Tim and Kathy a hand!" host Mark Johnson said, clapping his hands.

The seven year old twin brother and sister waved and skipped off the stage, wearing sequined costumes for their dance routine.

The band waited in the wing behind the curtains as the children ran to their mother for a hug. "Can we get Mr. Johnson's autograph now?" the little boy asked.

"I don't think now's a good time, Timmy," his mother said. She rolled her eyes at Josh. "They *love* this show," she said.

"Okay Fallow Wing, you're up next," a man with a clipboard and headphones said.

Mr. Johnson walked right past Timmy who held his ticket and pen up to eye level. Johnson stopped where the band stood waiting. "Okay, this is it," he said.

Josh smiled at Johnson, then nodded to the side at Timmy and Kathy. "Cute kids."

Johnson glanced over his shoulder, "Yeah, right." He walked to a lady with a makeup brush and posed as she dabbed at his flawless, tanned complexion.

"Hey Timmy.   See that guy?" Josh said, pointing at Tom.   "He's gonna be a big star one day."

Timmy scrunched his mouth.

"It's just like having a rookie card, you just never know."

"Hey *mis*ter," Timmy held his ticket and pen for Tom.   Tom smiled, took the ticket and pen, then signed.

"Okay, places!" the man with the clipboard said. The band walked through the curtain across the stage to their instruments as instructed earlier that day.

"And five, four, three, two, and one," the man with the clipboard said.   Johnson ran onto the stage to theme music and applause.

"This next group is from right here in Chicago, ladies and gentlemen," Johnson said to the audience.   "They write and play original songs. Give it up for The *Fallo Wing*!"

Tom blinked in the bright lights, playing his acoustic and singing the opening verses.

Del Boland

FOR THE MOMENT
(Track 3)

Hold on today
Cause its all we've got
and it's all we need
Don't want to hear
about your plans
or your skeletons you hide away
From the day to day
You go from reminiscing
to concerns about what you'll be missing
You drown in yesterday's sorrow
while dreaming about tomorrow
You run, run away
You run, run from today

Time –
can it freeze
for a moment
while I look at you
Seems these days ,
come a long, long way
misbelieving
that it's here to stay

Stop chasing all your hurries
Erase all your worries

Baker's Dozen

Everyday illusion
escalating your confusion
You run, run away
You run, run from today

Don't waste away my friend
in your bitter state
Just simplify your thoughts
like a child
Seems the weight
of the world can bring you down
But you need to shake it
and you can shake it with me
You go from reminiscing
to concerns about what you'll be missing
You drown in yesterday's sorrow
while dreaming about tomorrow
You run, run away
You run, run from today

Marilyn danced in the front seat as Josh drove through traffic. "We nailed it, we nailed it!" she sang.

"I don't know about *ya'll*," Darius said from the back seat, "but I'm thinking we *gotta* move to the next round."

"Yep," Austin agreed. Tom leaned against the door, behind Marilyn, basking in the afterglow. "Hi, isn't that Lech?" Tom said. "*Josh, stop* tha *car.*"

Josh pulled over at the curb and turned his head around. "Where?"

"Ova thare." Tom pointed.

Lech stood outside the fence of a school playground.

"I thought you were all kidding about him," Marilyn said.

Josh pressed the unlock button. "I should ask him if he needs a ride."

Before Josh could open his door, Lech ducked through an opening in a wooden fence.

Austin said. "I think we should sit on it for now."

CHAPTER TWENTY SEVEN

Austin glanced in both directions down the corridor then turned the doorknob to Lech's room. "*Sales* meeting?"

"Yeah," Darius responded, following Austin inside then closing the door behind.

Austin flipped a switch and fluorescent lights flickered on. "I'm not in sales," he mumbled through the bulge in his lower lip.

"A wise man once said, 'In a successful company, *everyone's* in sales.'"

Darius opened a dresser drawer and slid his hand underneath a nest of socks.

Austin raised the end of one pillow, then lowered it. Using one hand to lift the mattress, he swept the other hand under. "Here's something."

"Lemme see," Darius said.

Austin held a photo of a young girl posing on a blanket in a bikini at the beach. "Could be his daughter," he said.

"Lech never mentioned a daughter. And, why put it under the mattress?"

"No clue."

Josh waited for Rosie and Harv to sit along with the others as he stood at the front of the conference room next to the whirring projector.

"A couple of housekeeping items," Josh said. "Just a reminder, odd hours for the ladies in the showers, even hours for the guys. In every way possible, please respect each other's privacy."

Darius and Austin exchanged glances.

"What if we wanna shower together?" Harv asked.

Josh sighed. "I don't want to get into a long list of rules and exceptions here. Just keep it basic. If you want to shower together, fine. But, please use a little discretion or do it at your own risk. Fair enough?"

Harv nodded.

Janie played with white threads hanging from a hole in her jeans, her knees propped up. Tom tapped something on his phone and Drew looked at his watch.

"I don't like long, unnecessary meetings, so I'll try to keep it short. I think it's good for us to get together once a week to make sure everyone's informed."

"I hate meetings," Rosie murmured.

"Let's don't call them meetings," Janie offered.

"Sorry. But, let's just stick to an easy format. I make a few announcements, provide weekly numbers and we take a few minutes for discussion when needed. I'm thinking ten minutes on average."

Janie poked out her bottom lip.

Darius said, "Okay boss, we're at the five minute mark." Marilyn giggled.

"Sooooo, here we *are*." Josh advanced a slide showing a bar chart. "Sales are moving in the right direction. Folks are trying the new systems and we're getting some residual cash flow." Josh pointed at the progressive trend with his yardstick.

He changed slides. "Here's our income statement. The number at the bottom is our net income, which is now positive."

"*Yay!*" Drew cheered.

"Right. And the last slide," Josh pressed the remote, "is our balance sheet. I want to draw your attention to the Stockholder's Equity Line. For those of you participating in gain shares, this, in part, represents your investment in the company."

Josh picked up a stack of white envelopes and removed a rubber band before walking around the room handing them out. "Here's this week's checks. Your pay stub shows your net pay along with the value of your gain shares. You'll also notice a special line called total compensation. This number is the cumulative net pay and the present value of your investment added together."

Amid the tearing of envelopes, Josh said, "I hope the trend will continue, but our current marketing strategy is limited by our budget. As we grow, we'll invest more into a larger campaign which Darius is developing. Any questions?"

"So, Darius is actually *working*?" Austin teased.

A few folks laughed.

Darius said, "I'll have you know I've been on the phone with the folks at NAMM, talking to stores and getting some cheap ads for the short term. The website's looking good with a 4/10 Google rating and we're starting to see a few reviews in trade magazines."

"Hey," Rosie said, "Harv's total compensation's more than mine!"

"Glad you mentioned that, Rosie," Josh answered. "Harv went with Option A, so he earned wages and a portion of the profit."

"And, what about *your* pay?" Rosie asked, staring at Josh. A chair squeaked and someone coughed.

Josh opened his check. "Okay, let's have a look." Josh unfolded the payment stub. "Here's a line called executive bonus . . . hmmmm . . . two hundred grand . . . " He paused for effect. "Not bad for one week's work."

A chair squeaked. Darius drummed his fingers on the table.

"Ummmmm. Hell*loooo*?" Drew said. "He's *kid*ding," he sang.

"I also take part in Option A," Josh continued. "In full disclosure, I have a large stake in the company, so that portion of my total compensation will be more when sales are good."

"Figures," Rosie huffed.

"But, my pay is not that much higher than yours. I'm not getting a bonus or any form of compensation other than what's shown on this stub, which I'm happy to share with you." Josh handed his pay stub to Rex.

"Josh, you don't have to do that," Rex said, handing it back.

"It's all part of a quarterly report, so you'll all know the first week in January. It's not a secret."

"Well, I don't know about ya'll," Darius began, "but I can wait 'til January."

"Speakin' of January, I'm hungry," Harv said.

CHAPTER TWENTY EIGHT

Gene bit into a sandwich. "What's she makin'?" he mumbled.

"Dunno," Francis replied from his position on a five gallon bucket, staring at a monitor screen attached to a vertical rib support at the rear of the van. "She's been cutting wood and stacking it for days."

"Strange," Gene said.

"Yep."

"Wonder what all the windows are for?"

"Dunno," Francis replied.

Tap, tap, tap.

Gene and Francis looked at each other. "Was that you?" Francis asked.

"Nope."

Tap, tap, tap.

Gene asked, "What should we do?"

"Who is it?" Francis called.

"It's me, Janie," a muffled voice came from outside the van.

Francis reached toward the double doors on the side of the van and opened one wide enough to see Janie's upper body lean into view with a scarf wrapped tightly around her neck.

"Have either of you seen Freddie?"

Francis turned to Gene who shook his head. "Nope."

"Okay, thanks."

Lech braced himself near the top of a sixteen foot step ladder, adjusting a small security camera.

Standing at the bottom of the ladder, Janie asked, "Lech, have you seen Freddie?"

"No." Lech fiddled with a wing nut. "He just disappears sometimes. He'll come back."

"It's time for us to leave. I wanna take him to the Chicago Theater for the show."

"Check down in the basement. I saw him down there a few days ago."

"Okay."

CHAPTER TWENTY NINE

Raaaahhhhhhhh! Two chainsaws ran at full throttle beyond the curtain.

Backstage, where the band waited, a large monitor displayed a delayed scene from only fifty feet away. The image of a man continued to juggle on the screen, not matching the sound on stage as the chain saws thudded, puttering to a stall, then a collective "Oooooohhhhhhhhhhh!" from the live audience. The video feed switched to an ad for pain reliever, never showing the accident as several stagehands ran around the band members backstage, through the curtains.

"Okay," Josh said. "Looks like we're up next."

He peeked out at two men mopping the floor and the contestant -- his arm wrapped in a tourniquet -- ushered off the opposite side of the stage by a paramedic.

"I guess that's a good reason to delay the signal," Josh said.

At the wing, Janie stood with Freddie next to a man in a suit, waving her arms in the air, then pointing in their direction. The man followed Janie and Freddie across to where the band stood waiting for their introduction.

Janie clasped her hands tightly to her chest, smiling broadly, her golden eyes shimmering beneath her dark bangs. "This is Morris Goldblum. He owns a record company!"

Morris shook each of their hands as Janie bobbed and wriggled with excitement. She grinned at Tom and quickly nodded her head, her eyes wide.

"Good luck out there," Goldblum said. "I hope we can chat afterwards."

Darius grinned at the exec, slapping Austin on the back, out of view.

"Okay folks, you're on in ten," the man with the clipboard and headphones said, "Remember, don't say anything until you're asked."

"Now ladies and gentlemen," the emcee's voice came from the stage, "our home town favorites from last week are back. Please give a big Chicago welcome for The Fallow Wing!"

As instructed, the band filed onto the stage to applause and waited in front of their instruments. The judges would ask a few questions before their performance.

"Tom, it says here that you write your own songs," Roland Sizemore, a national radio personality, asked from behind a long table at which the three panel judges sat.

"Yes."

"You have a real gift for words, don't you?"

"Yes." The crowd laughed.

Del Boland

"So, says here you're also a professor at Columbia?"

"Yes, I teach songwritin' courses and help to organize several events throughout the year."

"Okay, so what are you playing tonight?"

"We're plyin' a song called 'Draimin' Out Loud.'"

"I can't wait to hear this song," Jennifer Jones, former singer for Ratsnake said. "They really blew me away last time."

DREAMING OUT LOUD
(Track 11)

Lick your wounds,
wash the frown away
Separate minds
with the same to say
When attacked
I retract into myself
Thinking you
are worlds away
Something linked
within the genes
Can't explain
things I truly mean
Wipe the dirt
from off my face
Heads and tails

Baker's Dozen

in the human race

CHORUS

We're saying different things
with the same words
And the way we deal
with the way we feel
can be so very different
And I can't understand
your subtleties cause
You're unlike me
cause I'm dreaming
I'm dreaming out,
I'm dreaming out loud

Canine in
a feline world
Barking endlessly
as it twirls
Wipe the dirt
from off my face
Heads and tails
in the human race

(CHORUS)

Janie's head bobbed with the music, her hands on Freddie's shoulders.

The crowd stood on their feet and cheered at the end of the song. The band gathered again in front of their instruments and waved. A few seconds later, they jogged off stage to where Janie, Freddie and Goldblum stood waiting.

"Awesome!" Janie tiptoed to kiss Tom.

Goldblum nodded. "I really like your sound."

"Thank you," Tom responded as self appointed spokesman for the band.

"I'm here to offer you a deal," Goldblum said. "But, I have a problem."

Darius furrowed his eyebrows. "Uh oh. There's *always* a problem."

"I'll just spell it out for you. I have studio time in L.A. I also have contacts with Kenny Ray who's looking for an opening act on his European tour."

Tom folded his arms and tilted his head slightly. "I don't git it."

"I need you right *now*," Goldblum said.

"You mane, after we're done with Talent USA?" Tom asked.

"No. I need you in the L.A. studio in six days."

Darius looked at Tom, then Goldblum. "What are the terms?"

"Standard terms. We pay you, as a band, a $50,000 advance."

Baker's Dozen

Darius said to Tom, "It's like a loan. Our portion of the sales revenue is used to pay it back. We begin receiving payments after the debt is paid."

Tom nodded. "Can we say the contract?"

"Sure." Goldblum pulled a thick envelope from inside of his jacket and handed it to Tom. "You have an important decision to make, but let me offer you something to think about. I've been around these shows. You have a choice between one bird in the hand or one bird in the bush."

"Isn't that two birds in a bush?" Austin asked.

"No. It's one bird," Goldblum said. "The winner of this competition gets a contract and a tour. I'm offering you a contract and a tour."

Tom rubbed his chin, taking stock of his bandmates. Song rights hadn't been discussed. He slapped his palm with the envelope. "Thank you. We all nade to thank about it for a bit."

"I need an answer tomorrow. Here's my card."

Goldblum answered his phone and walked toward the side exit.

"Oh. My. God." Janie said.

CHAPTER THIRTY

"Look Freddie!" Janie pointed to an elf family seated around a Christmas tree, one of many scenes in the decorated windows of Marshall Field's along State Street. Janie pulled the hood of Freddie's coat over his head as the first snow began to fall.

Freddie shouted, "Santa!" at the next window through which a molded plastic Saint Nick prepared to enter a chimney, frozen in mid stride, his sack thrown over his shoulder.

"Should I ask for more?" Tom asked.

Janie peeked out from under her bangs. "What do you mean?"

"I own the songs. Should I get more than the others?"

Freddie waved at Rudolph through a window.

"Didn't they help with the arrangements?" Janie asked.

"Well, yes."

"Don't you think you should share the credit and the royalties?"

An orderly flow of taxis, busses and cars moved along State.

"I'm thirsty," Freddie said.

"Hmmmmmm?" Tom turned back toward them. "What?"

"Freddie's thirsty. Actually, I'm a little thirsty, too."

"I know a plice," Tom said. "Lit's cross here."

They waited for the signal, then crossed State Street at Washington in a crowd of shoppers.

"Just keep goin' strite," Tom shouted from behind.

Away from State Street, they huddled together, walking in the shadows of the surrounding buildings on Washington, then crossed Dearborn to the Christkindlmarket. Tom stepped up to a food stand and ordered hot chocolates, blowing vapor into his hands, alternating his weight on his toes and heels. The vendor put lids on the steaming drinks and Tom dropped a ten on the counter. "Kipe the choinge."

Freddie sipped his hot chocolate, walking between Janie and Tom through the faux Christmas village erected each November at Daley Plaza. Bavarian music played as they meandered among other 'villagers' dressed in colorful knit caps and heavy sweaters -- some wearing lederhosen and Bavarian jackets.

Large flakes now dotted the overcast sky surrounding the collective glow from the booths selling handmade toys, hot pretzels, Belgian waffles, bratwurst and beer -- a contrast of warm light and cool, blue darkness that reminded Janie of a Thomas Kinkade painting.

Tom held Goldblum's card, reading his name, phone numbers and website, all listed under an attractive LA RECORDS logo. "I nade to check this goy out."

"I think he's legit," Janie said. "He seemed very nice."

"I don't think noice is the word I'd use."

Freddie stared at a wooden toy with fan blades spinning above four lit candles. Beneath the blades, two carved wooden deer appeared to run in a circle around small trees arranged in the center.

Janie flashed her golden puppy dog eyes at Tom, who reached for his wallet.

"Wanna tike a buggy roid?" Tom asked, handing his credit card to the vendor.

"I don't know. Maybe we should get back."

Tom signed and returned his card to his billfold.

Freddie's eyes widened as Janie presented the treasure, spinning slowly atop her open hands. He stood, mesmerized by the motion of the toy, his mouth open. She said, "Take it, it's yours."

Squeezing his hands together against his chest, Freddie shook his head, tears streaming down his face.

"Freddie? What's wrong?"

"You hold it. I'll break it."

Baker's Dozen

Exiting the market, they weaved past a few cherub faced revelers in alpine hats, singing a bier haus song.

Freddie tugged at Janie's arm and pointed.

"Mama!" he shouted. Across the sidewalk, a woman sat wrapped in a soiled quilt, rattling change in a rusty coffee can.

"Freddie! No!" Janie called.

The woman rattled her can at Freddie as he approached, his arms held wide. She leaned back, focusing her eyes.

"It's me, Mama!" Freddie leaned over, wrapping his arms around the blanketed woman.

"Mama, what's wrong with your legs?"

"It's okay, baby."

On the other side of the sidewalk, Janie watched, leaning her head against Tom's chest, holding the extinguished wooden carousel in her hand.

Freddie wriggled his hand into his pocket.

Janie asked, "What's he doing?"

Tom moved across, next to Freddie who pulled out a crisp one hundred dollar bill, folded in half. Tom snatched the money away from Freddie's hand as the woman's trembling fingers reached up.

"No!" Freddie said. "Give it to Mama!"

"I'll give it to 'er when she stands up," Tom said with resolve, tucking the bill into his folded arms.

"This is my corner," the woman said in a low, raspy voice.

Janie called from behind, "Tom." He glanced over his shoulder at Janie shaking her head at him.

"Okye, foin," Tom said, returning his attention to the woman. "Just tell me tha truth. Kin ya walk?"

"Yes," the woman murmured.

Tom handed her the money. Her fingers trembled as she curled the bill into her fist before quickly retracting the prize inside her quilt.

"Freddie." A cough rattled deep inside her chest. "Where've you been, baby? Mama misses you so much."

"I live at the warehouse."

"Where?"

"At the warehouse with Josh. You can live there too, Mama."

A man wearing a heavy black overcoat over a gray suit walked slowly toward them. He leaned over and dropped a five into the woman's can. "My sister's boy's autistic," he said, patting Freddie on the shoulder. "I know how hard it can be."

Tom smiled and nodded at the man.

"Freddie, you wanna stay here with Mama for a while?"

"Yes."

"Okye. Ya know what?" Tom said, his mouth now drawn into a thin line. "I've sane enough. C'mon Freddie."

"No. I wanna stay with Mama."

"What's your name?" Janie asked the woman.

"Annie."

"Annie, it's okay," Janie said. "Please stand up."

Bracing with one hand, Annie turned onto her knees. Unsteadily, she rose to her feet, her quilt still draped over her shoulders.

Janie touched the woman's hand. "Come with us."

CHAPTER THIRTY ONE

The high back on Josh's office chair swiveled from side to side. "Okay," he said on his phone, "I'll be in touch."

He turned and scribbled something on a notepad.

Janie cleared her throat.

"C'mon in," Josh said without looking.

"There's someone here to see you," Janie said, standing with Annie at his open door. Josh turned in his chair, then leaned back slowly and scratched the back of his head.

"Hello Annie," he said.

"Hello Mr. Baker."

Janie asked, "You know each other?"

Annie and Josh both nodded.

Josh said, "We've met a few times, actually." Rising from his chair he stepped around, wrapping an arm around her shoulder, leading her to one of two guest chairs near the front of his desk. "Please sit down."

Annie sat. Josh laid a hand on her shoulder and sat at the edge of the other guest chair, assessing her condition. "Janie, please close the door and sit down," he said, his eyes still focused on Annie.

The door creaked and latched. Janie padded across the room, but hesitated, unsure of where to sit. "Just use my chair," Josh said, still taking stock of Annie.

"Where've you been?" he asked.

She lowered her head, shaking it slowly from side to side.

Josh said, "Freddie's doing very well."

"I know. I saw him."

Josh curled his lower lip under, then pressed it forward against his teeth, feeling it scrape across. He eyed her, his lips now pursed.

"Annie. What happened with the job?"

She shook her head.

"Did they treat you well?"

She nodded slowly. "Business was bad," she murmured.

Josh gently chewed his lower lip for a moment. "I want you to go with Janie. Get cleaned up."

"Thank you."

Josh held her arm as she lifted herself from the chair. "Janie," Josh said, walking slowly alongside Freddie's mother, "please ask Rex to get something for Annie to eat."

"I can fix something for her."

"You have plenty to do. We don't want to upset Rex."

LA RECORDS displayed at the top of Tom's computer screen. Freddie sat across from him on the edge of his bed. Tom clicked the word "Clients" listed as part of the menu at the bottom of the page.

A few of the artists were familiar to him. He saw photos of Mr. Goldblum standing with his arm around them, his large teeth gleaming.

Tom dialed his phone and waited.

"Where's Mama?"

"Don't worry," Tom said, waiting for an answer. "She'll be back."

"Diane. Tom."

Tom nodded his head, acknowledging a response.

He said, "Do you know anyone at LA Records?"

Tom pushed a paper clip with his pen along the top of his desk.

"So, they've bin aroun' for a while?"

He laid the pen next to the paper clip.

"Okye. Good. Thoinks."

Freddie said, "I'm hungry."

"Okye Freddie, just wite a few minutes. We'll go down and fine somethin' in the fridge."

Tom dialed the phone again.

"You want some spaghetti?" Rex asked.

"That would be nice, thank you," Annie answered.

Janie sat next to her in the break room. "So, where did you work?"

"Gary Steel," Annie said.

"What did you do for them?"

The woman's head lifted, her dark eyes sparkling with dignity. "I was Associate Director of Human Resources."

Harvey's overalls and hairy chest appeared at the open doorway. "Watcha cookin'?" he asked, peering from beneath the header.

Annie's mouth dropped open. She pointed, her eyes wide with terror.

"Oh, that's just Harv," Janie said. He ducked through the opening.

"It ain't for you Meatloaf," Rex growled, standing on a chair, waiting on the microwave.

Harvey pointed. "Who's the bum?"

"Harvey!" Janie blurted. "Annie, don't let him scare you. He's like that with everybody."

"You still dressed as a mutant, chainsaw killer?" Rex asked.

"No," Harv said, looking down at himself. "What's wrong with this?"

"Nothing, if you recently escaped from a prison psych ward."

Harvey tried to latch the loose strap over his hairy shoulder. He tugged hard and clipped it over a large brass button, which popped from the tension. The button rolled under the fridge. "See whatcha' made me do?"

"I know somebody who makes circus tents," Rex said. "Maybe he could make you an XXXXL muumuu. Actually, I think you'd look nice in a jacket with the arms tied around the back."

"Funny."

"Yeah, it's a gift."

Janie held Annie close, hands on her shoulders

Harv stared at the trembling woman. "There's not enough meat on her bones to make a decent pot roast."

"Harvey, please go do something," Janie said, glaring at him. "You're scaring her."

CHAPTER THIRTY TWO

"So, this is the shop."

Annie wore a mid length, gray wool skirt with a wide black belt and a silky, lilac blouse.

Earlier, Janie had talked about her father while trimming the woman's hair neatly and painting her fingernails pink in Annie's new room.

Ten feet away, Rosie furrowed her brow at them, stacking several pieces of sawn wood. Harvey stepped out of the tool shed, waving his fingers like a child.

Janie guided Annie gently by the arm, away from the spectacle of Harvey's butt crack as he leaned over to lift something from the shop floor. Perhaps in an effort to improve his ax murderer image, Harvey had changed into a Bears warm up suit that was two sizes too small. "Maybe the overalls were not such a bad idea, after all," Janie whispered as they walked away. Annie giggled.

"This is Marilyn's area where she makes stained and beveled glass." A partially completed, beveled glass panel rested flat under a ventilated hood on a neatly organized shop table next to a small torch.

"Where is she?"

"She's around somewhere."

"I want her to see me in the skirt and blouse she gave me."

Nearby, Drew lowered the Baker Electronics banner, securing it in place. The truck was parked between Harv's bike and Josh's Range Rover against the far wall. Darius had parked his BMW on the other side of Josh.

"So, they dress as clowns?" Annie asked.

"Kinda scary, actually."

They walked slowly toward the office, Janie pointing to the brick walls surrounding them, explaining the improvements they'd made to the old building.

Arriving at the office building, Janie opened the door for Annie, leading her past the break room to the double doors of the production area through which they saw Josh, Austin and Marilyn soldering components at a work bench.

Janie motioned for Annie to follow. She whispered, "Marilyn will see you later. I don't want to disturb them right now," then continued down the corridor through another set of double doors, into the auditorium.

"Wow," Annie said, looking around.

On the stage, Darius, Rex, Tom, and Freddie relaxed on the furniture in the warm glow from two table lamps, like a scene in a play. Behind them, Harv and Rosie had built two sections of faux wall on which they'd hung a few pictures. White chair railing separated the upper, gold colored wallpaper from the white paneled wainscoting on the lower half of the walls. Crimson curtains flanked one of Marilyn's beveled glass windows. Through the window, indirect lighting drew attention to a winter scene of snow on trees, a painting on canvas. In the center of a second wall which completed an interior corner, an electronic flame flickered in the hearth of a large fireplace below a mantle, helping to complete the image.

"Where's the film maker?"

"Lech." Janie arched her eyebrows. "We're always asking that question. I don't know."

CHAPTER THIRTY THREE

REC flashed in red at the top right corner of the viewfinder as Lech walked around the stage. Wearing a blue skirt, Marilyn leaned over the relocated conference table, arranging silverware around thirteen place settings of her Grandmother's Wedgwood china. "Nice," Lech said. She smirked over her shoulder at him, smoothing the back of her skirt with her hand. Janie pressed new white candles into Marilyn's sterling silver candlestick holders while Annie folded cloth napkins.

Lech put his camera down to help Rosie carry covered trays from a cart at the bottom of the steps to another table on the opposite side of the stage, also with a tablecloth.

Josh walked through the doors at the back of the room, followed by the other men, all dressed neatly in slacks and button down shirts.

Rosie poured red wine from a large decanter into Waterford crystal glasses on a silver tray, also supplied by Marilyn, who placed two loaves of freshly baked sourdough bread into silver baskets, setting them at opposite ends of the table.

Baker's Dozen

Janie used a long lighter to light the four equally spaced candles on the table as Rosie balanced the tray, placing the glasses half filled with wine at each place setting.

Mounting the stage, Josh lifted a chair and carried it to the long side of the table closest to the edge.

"Wait a minute, Josh," Lech said. "I'd like to get a picture of all of us."

Josh held the chair chest high, waiting on instructions.

"Let's arrange all the chairs on the back side of the table," Lech said. "After I get the shot, we can put them all around."

"Sounds good to me." Josh carried the chair to the other side of the table. Austin and Harvey carried more chairs, following his lead.

Lech stood near the edge of the stage, his Nikon attached to a tripod which he held folded in his hand. "Okay, please. I'd like everyone to sit behind the table. Josh, you sit in the middle."

Footsteps reverberated through the hall from the hollow stage floor as each found a place at the table for the photo. Lech extended the legs of the tripod, then peered through the viewfinder. "Okay, let's do a few practice shots."

"I'm wearin' a pair of Janie's thong underwear," Tom announced through a rare smile.

"That's not a pleasant image," Darius said, grinning.

"Okay, big smile . . . and . . . ," the camera clicked.

"Good. Let's do one more for fun."

"Taking pictures makes me hungry," Harvey said.

"Breathing makes you hungry," Rosie said, forcing her normally scowling mouth into a thin line.

"Okay . . . and," the camera clicked again.

"This time, I want everyone to stay in position. I'll run over to get into the picture."

Lech set the timer which began to flash, waiting to count down at the touch of a button.

"Is everyone ready?" he called, still looking at the camera.

"Yeeessssss," they whined in unison.

"When I count to three, I'll start the timer and move behind Darius. Okay, one,"

"I have to go to the bathroom," Freddie said.

"Just wait Freddie," Janie said.

"I have gas."

"Just hold it," Janie said again through her teeth.

"I can't."

"Two . . .," Lech said.

Squeeeeee - bbrrrrriiiiiiipppppppphhhh!

"Nice," Darius said, still posing for the shot.

"Three."   Lech pressed the button and scampered to his position behind Darius, waiting on the timer."

"Oh, dear God," Darius said seconds before the camera clicked.

Josh stood up. "I need some fresh air."

They moved away from a giggling Freddie, all waving their hands in front of their faces. "Excuse me," Freddie said.

After walking back to the camera, Lech viewed an odd representation of horror, disgust, and mirth displayed on their faces in the photo.

Rosie used a lid from one of the serving dishes, helping to move the air around the table, her grimacing face turned away.

"Brats? We're having brats?" Austin asked, inspecting the exposed contents of the serving dish.

"What's wrong with brats?" Rex rasped.

"Not complainin'. Just not what I'd call the traditional feast, that's all."

"You want traditional feast?" the little man growled. "Go to the 'burbs. Here, you get what I fix, or you go hungry."

"I'm tickled pink," Darius said. "Just this mornin', my stomach gurgled. I swear, it said, 'Bratwurst.'"

"Alright folks, just a few things," Josh edged closer to the group from the corner of the stage where he'd taken refuge, testing the air as he went.

"The numbers look great. We saw a 35% increase in sales this week."

Josh waited for light applause to subside.

"And, I'm happy to say . . . "

He checked each of their faces, removing the rubber band from the stack of white envelopes. " . . . we're all getting a little bonus."

"Yay!" Drew shouted.

Darius lifted a glass from the table. "Let's have a toast." He waited as the others rustled around him, finding wine glasses. "A lot has happened these past few months," he began. "The band signed with LA Records yesterday!"

"Outstanding!" Austin said.

"So," Darius continued, "I'd like to thank the band, especially Tom, for all the hard work."

"Cheers!" Tom said, sipping his wine. "Cheers," came a response from the group.

"Also, I want everyone to know that I'm a lucky man. I needed you more than you know. Each and every one of you . . . ,"

"Cheers," Freddie said.

" . . . aannnddddd," Darius interrupted, "I want to thank everyone for all your contributions at Baker Electronics."

Josh said, "Hear, hear!" They raised their glasses again.

"Finally, I'd especially like to thank Mr. Joshua Baker, without whom, none of this would be possible!"

"Woo, hoooo!" Austin and Marilyn chimed together. "Cheers!" and "Thanks Josh!" mixed with the clinking of glasses. Janie wiped under her eye with a finger, noticing Freddie leaning against Annie across the table.

Josh said, "May I say one more thing, that is, before Rex carves the . . . uh . . . bratwurst." He waited for everyone to lower their glasses. "I'm honored to be part of this enterprise."

"You?" Darius said.

"Seriously. I'm truly honored and I find great reward working together with such a fine group of folks. I mean that with all my heart."

Janie blew her nose.

"Thanks to all of you for everything that *you* do."

"To Baker's dozen," Marilyn toasted. "Salute!"

CHAPTER THIRTY FOUR

A low groan accompanied the distant sound of trains in the relative darkness, followed by the rustling of sheets.

"Tom, what's wrong?" Janie murmured.

"No, no, no!"

Seated at his desk, Tom removed his round glasses and pinched the slight crook in his long thin nose. He laid the glasses on the desk and leaned over his propped arms, pressing his face from side to side in open hands.

Janie lifted herself, stretching her neck to see Tom's computer screen, the only source of light in the room displaying an error message.

He lowered his head further, hands sliding up his face, through his tousled hair on both sides then clasping his fingers around the back of his head. The groan became a soft wail.

Janie swung her legs over the side of the bed, sitting and placing one hand on his shoulder. "I don't understand."

"It was all a scam."

"What?"

"The website, the receptionist, the card!" He sat up in the chair.

Janie slid forward, standing and leaning over Tom, her arms over his shoulders, folded around his chest, her cheek pressed against his, staring at the screen.

"The website's gone," he said. "I searched LA Records and found this." Tom pecked a few keys. A different screen appeared. "It's paht of a conglomerate, appearin' low in the search results. They're not very big."

"What happened to their site?"

"It was a spoof. I used the URL on Goldblum's cahd."

"You called."

"The phone number's now out of service."

"That can't be! You talked to Diane."

"LA Records is legit. I'm sich a drongo!"

"What about the check?" Janie asked.

"He said it would transfer at midnight. I checked it.," Tom said. "Nothin'."

"What about the contract?"

Tom wriggled free of Janie's arms. He reached into a small trash can beneath his desk, retrieving a ball of paper, unraveling it and smoothing it on the desk.

"Piper! Crumpled piper! That's all this is!" Tom slapped the back of his open hand down against the wrinkled stack. "Worthless! We got nothin'."

Grabbing the contract, Tom ripped it in half, then wadded it again into a ball. Squeaking back in his chair, he threw it wildly against the ceiling, the ball of paper separating, landing in pieces on the carpet.

"What about Talent USA?"

He stood abruptly, facing her. "We withdrew. It was a condition of the freakin', phony contract! It was all paht of a plan! Probably one of our competitors, we'll *nev*-uh know for sure! That guy! That guy that *you* met. He got what he wanted!"

Janie collapsed against the wall next to the bed, sliding down, sitting on the floor. She raised her knees to her chest and hummed. Her Aunt Irene's voice called to her from the kitchen door, holding a phone against her apron.

"Oh grite! That's jist grite Janie!"

"What?"

"I need ya here with *mae*, okye?"

"Okay," she whispered.

"Sich a classic scam. The urgency, leaving little toim for us to kitch on. I'm sich a drongo!"

"I was so happy for you," she sobbed. "He . . . I . . . ," Janie's voice trailed.

Tom snatched his shirt from the back of the chair. "I'm done!" He jabbed one arm through a sleeve, walking toward the door in his pajama bottoms. He opened the door, a dark silhouette against the lighted corridor, then thrust the other arm into his shirt. "Thoinks!" he shouted, stepping into the hallway, slamming the door behind him.

CHAPTER THIRTY FIVE

Golden mist hovered low over Lake Michigan in the distance, the sun peaking halfway over the horizon. He'd earned the office with a view. It comforted him to prop his feet, still in house slippers, on the wooden chair which faced from the wall next to the window. Scores of students had squirmed in the seat over the years, usually asking for some reprieve. He'd always worked with them, helping them to adjust to the rigors of study in a particularly non-conducive environment. He'd seen them regularly at the bars, some playing open mikes.

He understood. At least, he once understood. He'd followed a similar pattern. For the first time, the stress of student life at Columbia seemed less significant to him. After all, failing a class can serve a greater purpose, instilling a new sense of commitment for some, while sometimes delivering a hard lesson to others.

You must love what you do, he'd frequently told them. It's not about money. It should never be about the money. It's about music resonating deep within the soul, yearning to find a voice or a sound.

Many of his colleagues had lost their way, seeking stardom outside the relative comfort of tenure. Why? Why ruin a perfectly good life in pursuit of the unattainable? Why not accept a comfortable existence?

He wrote the last line of a lyric on a slip of paper and stuffed it into his shirt pocket, then lowered his legs from the chair, still in black pajamas dotted with sepia colored images of famous songwriters. Perhaps it wasn't a good idea to shuffle around in nightclothes, even on a Saturday morning.

Darius half laid on the couch, his head propped against the arm, staring at the ceiling. Marilyn leaned forward in a chair, resting her face in one hand, her arm on her knee. Austin half sat against the arm of Marilyn's chair, his hands on his thighs.

The double doors squeaked open. Tom eased through and shuffled down the aisle with his head lowered, hands stuffed in the pockets of his PJs.

"What do we say to him?" Marilyn whispered.

"Let me handle it," Darius said. "Yo, Tom. What up, bro?"

"You git the news?" Tom asked.

"Well. Yeah. We know."

"Where is she?" Tom asked.

Marilyn glanced up at Darius, eyebrows arching, creating wrinkles in the center of her forehead.

Darius nodded reassurance at her before answering him. "She's gone, Tom. She packed that suitcase she calls a purse and hauled her skinny ass out the door."

"Nice work, Darius," Marilyn said in a low voice.

"Tom, yo, it's all gonna work out."

"Yee-uh, roit."

"We'll go independent. I'll help set up a website and we'll start working it local."

"I'm worried about 'er," Tom said.

Marilyn nodded. "Yeah, me too."

"Man." Austin sighed. "I can't believe it."

Tom scuffed a slipper against the wooden floor of the stage. "I'm a dipstick."

"Dude," Darius said, "you're right. You're a dipstick."

Marilyn cleared her throat.

"But, we're right there with you. We're all dipsticks."

Tom picked up his acoustic from a stand. "No. It's my fault. I should've known. I've been down this road once before."

He played a few chords, then plopped into the empty chair, throwing one leg over the arm, his guitar held at an angle.

He hummed and played a few more chords, then lowered the guitar to the floor, leaning it against the chair. He retrieved the paper and pen from his pocket and scribbled a few notes.

"Watch'a writin'?" Austin drawled.

Tom scowled, scratched out a word then wrote a new one above it. "It's a song I wrote this mornin'."

He scratched out another word and pressed the end of the pen to the corner of his mouth. "I kinda wrote it in the moment. Blowin' off a little stame."

"Some great songs were written in the moment, dawg. Let's have a look at it."

Tom handed Darius the paper.

"Who's this about?" Darius asked.

"The "you" in the song is the world."

"Phew!" Darius said. "For a minute there, I thought you were breaking up with me."

Marilyn cleared her throat.

Tom lifted the guitar and played a few more chords.

"Kinda soft, like a slow rhumba?" Darius asked.

"Yee-uh, that's what I'm thankin'."

Darius leaned forward and handed the paper to Marilyn. "Ya'll wanna give it a shot?"

I'LL NEVER UNDERSTAND
(Track 13)

Midnight
under the moonlight
Gazing up
at a starry sky

Baker's Dozen

I'm wondering
if the world I know
is the world it seems
Now somebody's got to know
Take me from this dream
it's just some that I've deemed
to be key to me
Don't be leading me on

Cry for what you did
Repent for what you said
But the path left behind
sheds some light
on the road ahead
Yeah, I may never understand you

Midday
back in the boardroom
They wage it up
trying to cage the sky
Wondering if the world they know
is as gullible as it seems
Take me from your page
you did not account for rage
that's inside of me
You didn't confide in me

Cry for what you did

Del Boland

Repent for what you said
But the path left behind
sheds some light on the road ahead
Yeah, I may never understand you

CHAPTER THIRTY SIX

Annie and Harv stood side by side, watching Josh in the production area. "Okay, it's easy," Josh said. "The controls are on this tablet." He pointed at the electronic tablet hanging by a strap over his head and shoulder. Raising it, he showed Annie the touchscreen. "These buttons are numbered." Josh pressed button number one on the touchscreen and a cart moved along a programmed path. The cart slowed then stopped automatically at the end of the conveyor. He pressed button number two and forks supporting a fresh pallet lifted. He lowered the tablet to his side and slid boxed mixer units down rollers onto the pallet, arranging them tightly.

Annie tilted her head, peering at the pneumatics beneath the transport/lift. Her eyes followed the hose and power cord extending as a single wound snake to a spool mounted on the wall. The hose connected the lift to a compressor and tank in the corner of the production area and the power cord plugged into a socket. "This must cost a lot of money."

"Not really," Josh said, waving them back. "Harvey and I built it."

Harv said, "I welded. He did everything else."

"Next, you press button number three." Josh pressed the screen and the pallet lowered. An electric motor whirred as the pallet rotated ninety degrees.

Josh said, "You slide the next row of boxes down the conveyor, across the top of the first row." He demonstrated, arranging the second tier of boxes in alignment with the edges of the lower grouping. He repeated the sequence five times, stacking boxes into successive rows onto the pallet.

In the corner, the compressor cycled on, replenishing air inside the storage tank to ninety pounds, then rattled to a stop.

"The next part might be a little tricky." Josh pressed button number nine on the touch screen. The cart moved back several feet.

"You take the end of the plastic wrap around two corners of the stack." Josh tugged at one end of a roll of plastic, mounted vertically against the wall. He tightly wrapped it around, then pressed the adhesive edge of the plastic onto the boxes. "Now, you step back beyond this yellow line on the floor and press button number ten."

Josh pressed and the platform rotated two times then clicked. He moved back to the roll. "Now, pull until the end of the plastic sheet releases and then wrap it." He pulled the plastic sheet until it slipped away from the spool, then walked in the opposite direction,   pressing the clinging plastic down.

"I think I can do that," Annie said.

"Don't worry," Josh said.   "Harvey will be with you the first few times. The next part's easy."

Josh used button controls on the handle to guide the motorized pallet jack backwards through the door. Pressing another button, he maneuvered forward,   dragging the spring wound cable and hose through the open doors at the end of the corridor into the warehouse where Harv stood at the top of a ramp.

Harvey hopped down from the ramp dock and lowered the gleaming red tailgate of a pick up with Baker Electronics logos printed on both doors. The lowered gate and the ramp formed a flat surface over which Josh drove onto the lined bed of the truck then used a button to extend the forks and lower the pallet down before backing out.

"That's it," he said.

Darius leaned over the guard rail of the mezzanine and shouted down.   "Got a call from Music Universe! They're wanting their shipment!"

"Tell 'em it's coming!" Josh shouted back.

"I need you up here!" Darius yelled. He paced in a circle then pulled his phone out of his pocket.

Doodle link!   Josh fished out his phone and read the text. *We've got a bigger problem.*

Josh glanced up at Darius, who jabbed a finger in the direction of Tom's room.

Taking the steps two at a time, Josh met Darius at the top. "Tom?" he surmised.

"Yeah."

Josh and Darius paused outside the corridor.

"What is it?" Josh asked.

"The dude's hanging on by a thread."

"I know he's upset about the deal and Janie."

"There's more," Darius said. "The Fallow Wing website has been spoofed."

"What?"

"I'm getting calls from our so-called customers," Darius used his fingers to make quotes around customers. "They're saying they haven't received their merchandise."

"I don't recall any orders for merchandise."

"That's because we haven't received any," Darius' head tilted to one side, his eyes angled toward Josh.

"Oh no."

"'Oh no' is right," Darius said. "Somebody's taking orders under our name and not delivering."

Josh forced a smile. "Their profit margins must be ridiculous."

"How can you kid around at a time like this?"

Josh stared up at the ceiling for a moment. He sighed then opened the door for Darius.

"We need to take the site down," Josh said, leading the way through the corridor toward Tom's room. He stopped and tapped on Tom's door.

"It's open!" Tom called from inside.

Austin shouted at Darius and Josh from the opposite end of the hallway, "What's going on?"

Josh motioned for Austin to follow then stepped inside Tom's room.

"C'mon in," Darius said as Austin approached. "Close the door behind you."

Standing next to Tom, Josh asked, "Can you see the spoof site?"

"Yee-uh, it's roit here," Tom answered.

Darius stared at the screen for a moment. "Jesus, it looks just like ours."

"Not exactly." Josh pointed to the bottom of the screen.

Tom leaned back in his chair, staring over his round glasses. "An 800 numba? *Really*?"

Austin turned toward Darius, his eyes wide. "What do you do when *this* happens?"

"Dunno," his old friend said. "It's never happened to me before."

"Can't we *call* somebody?" Austin asked.

"Now, *that*, dear sir, I *do* know," Darius began. "Yes, we can call and we can file a complaint. A mild form of Cease and Desist will be issued -- a cyber slap on the wrist -- asking the violating party to please stop the fraud."

"Oh boy. I don't like where this is going," Josh murmured.

"So, the violating party changes the URL," Darius added, "and the spoof site pops up in three more places."

Austin narrowed his eyes. "Who has the time to do this sort of thing?"

"It's mostly Eastern Europe and Asia," Tom answered.

"Don't we have *laws* or something?" Austin asked.

Darius grinned and rapidly nodded his head. "Oh yeah," he said. "The Digital Millennium Copyright Act is all over it."

"He's bein' sarcastic," Tom said. "We have nothin'. The DMCA helped fuel internet commerce in the lite 80's."

"That's not a bad thing," Austin surmised.

"Yeah, but on the flip side," Darius began, "they pulled all the teeth out of our laws that protect intellectual property. There's no real chain of responsibility, so the internet service providers have no liability."

"Correct," Tom said. "They can block a site, but that's about it. We have little or no recourse."

Josh dialed his phone.

Darius gave him an incredulous side glance. "Wha chu doin'?"

"I'm calling it," Josh said.

"You think we might be showing our hand?" Austin asked.

Josh replied, "I'd say they don't really care if they're bold enough to list their phone number." He listened as the number patched through to an international line, then pressed speaker phone so the others could hear.

Baker's Dozen

"Thank you for calling Fallow Wing Store," a woman's voice answered in a thick Russian accent.

"Hi," Josh began, "I'd like to order a cd and two Fallow Wing t-shirts."

"May I please have name and credit card number?"

"Vladimir Putin," Josh said.

"Please, let me connect you to Service Department."

"Seriously?" Darius said through the side of his crooked mouth, his eyebrows forming a pyramid.

Josh shrugged.

Their original music played on the line as they waited.

"What's goin' on?" Tom murmured. "The whole world's tryin' to destroy The Fallow Wing."

"Hello," a man answered, also with a Russian accent. *"This is Wanda."*

"C'mon," Josh said. "Your name's Wanda?"

"Nyet. My real name cannot pronounce in English. No vowels. Besides, the mere mention of it destroy internet."

"Ah. A sense of humor," Josh replied. "Good."

"How can I help you, Mr. Baker?"

"Take down the Fallow Wing site."

"You Americans, all alike. Just like Reagan. 'Mr. Gorbachev . . . take down that wall,'" Wanda said with a surprisingly good Ronald Reagan impersonation.

"Hilarious."

"Da. No worry. I take down right away."

"That's it?" Josh said.   "I call your service department and you simply agree?"

"Of course not.   You must pay small service fee."

"How much?"

"One thousand American dollars wired to bank in Minsk."

"That's comforting," Josh said.

"You have my word."

CHAPTER THIRTY SEVEN

Freddie lay on his stomach, watching a toy train clicking around wrapped presents below a seven foot, live Christmas tree. Marilyn and Annie had decorated the outer branches of the tree with cd's and small plastic reproductions of guitars, drums and congas. Deeper inside the tree, they'd arranged an assortment of shiny trinkets used to promote the band and the business.

The tree rested in a large planter pot near the inside corner of the faux walls on the stage. A few feet away, the electronic flame flickered in the fireplace, gently blowing heat into the area.

From center stage, Marilyn and Tom sang carols, playing congas and acoustic guitar accompanied by Darius on an old cello he'd purchased online.

The door creaked.

"Get ready," Marilyn whispered.

"Happy Birthday to you!" they sang and played together, the others joining in as Josh mounted the steps, grinning with his arms outstretched to absorb the moment.

"Happy birthday to you!

Happy birthday dear Joosssshhhhhh!
Happy birthday to you!"

"And many more," Darius sang, oscillating his bow on an A note.

"Thank you all, so much." Josh said.

"How oooolllld are *you*?" Marilyn sang, winking at Josh.

"Um," he said. "I've lost count."

Josh sat next to Rosie and Harvey on the couch. Drew, Rex, Austin and Annie played dominoes on a predominately black and red oriental rug. Lech slumped in a chair, fiddling with his camera on his lap.

"What's up, Lech?" Josh asked. "You haven't said two words the whole week."

Lech shook his head.

Darius said, "School's out for the holidays."

Lech inhaled and exhaled loudly.

Josh narrowed his eyes at Darius with a quick shake of his head.

"So, what's goin' on in the world?" Austin asked, changing the subject from his cross-legged position on the floor.

"It ain't pretty," Rosie said.

"You gotta wonder what's wrong with folks these days," Harv added. "Everybody's raging."

"Yeah, tell me about it," Annie responded from her position on the floor in her new dark blue slacks and red sweater. She leaned on one arm, her striped sock feet neatly tucked against her butt. She'd put on weight and had regained some of her strength. Her smooth, chestnut colored face and straight white teeth masked her age and suffering.

"Hey, check this out!" Rex said. He extended his thirty four inch body along the floor of the stage and flipped a toggle switch on the side of a metal box. A pattern of lighted snow flakes traveled slowly down the darkened walls surrounding them. For a moment, only the clicking of the toy train accompanied the whirring motor inside the device as everyone except Lech seemed to enjoy the tranquil scene.

"I think it's time for hot chocolate." Rosie used her hand on Harv's leg to lift herself from the couch.

"Yay!" Drew said.

Josh leaned to one side and pulled a stack of square envelopes out of his back pocket. "I want to go ahead and give these to you."

He passed the stack around, then leaned back. Rosie brought him cocoa in a Spode Christmas cup.

Marilyn opened her card first. She read the card then walked from her stool and kissed Josh on the cheek. "Thank you," she whispered in his ear.

The others opened their cards, one at a time, each thanking Josh.

"Hey. I got a little something for ya'll," Drew said. He turned and lifted an empty, Jack Daniels cardboard box from behind him, then passed it around. "Everybody take one."

Rex reached inside the box and retrieved a Santa hat with Baker Electronics printed in silver glitter across the white fur. "Thanks." Rex put on his hat and passed the box.

"I thought we were having a gift exchange?" Harv said.

Marilyn pointed at an assortment of wrapped presents encircled by train tracks under the tree. "We are. We all select a number and take a gift. When it gets to you, you may choose from the tree or from someone else, surrendering your turn to them."

"Right," Rex said.

Marilyn opened a plastic bag, dumping slips of paper into the empty box. She said, "Okay, so everyone pick a number." She lowered the container to where Lech remained slumped in his chair. "Don't open your number yet, let everyone pick first."

Lech reached inside the box and rattled his hand around, sifting through the folded slips of paper before retrieving one. Marilyn held the box in front of Josh and curtsied. Sitting up, he selected a number. One by one, she moved around the stage, everyone selecting a number, then she took the last slip and placed the box on the floor.

"Okay, everyone," she said. "You can open them now."

"Yay, I'm number one!" Drew shouted, still sitting on the floor with his legs folded to one side wearing a red, one piece flannel, complete with trap door. He lifted himself then crossed the stage.

"Idiot," Rex grumbled. "Number one in this game is not good."

Standing at the tree, Drew bent over then reached a hand around, placing it over his trap door. "No peeking!" he said before lifting the largest box and returning to his spot on the floor.

"Go ahead, open it," Marilyn said. Drew removed a glittering silver bow attached to a matching ribbon around the green foil present. Marilyn said, "I'll take that." She placed the bow and ribbon into the same cardboard box she'd used to distribute the numbers.

Drew tore the green foil wrapping from the box and handed it to Rosie who stood waiting with a contractor's plastic trash bag, having finished her hot chocolate rounds.

He unfolded the flaps on the box and peered inside at wadded balls of newspaper. "Oh no. It's one of those box inside a box thingies."

Drew unwrapped each layer, finally ending up with a flat square wrapped in red paper at the end.

"Open it," Marilyn coaxed.

"That's what you said thirty minutes ago," he whined. "I'm exhausted. It's time for my nap."

Drew removed the last wrapping, revealing a set of bass guitar strings in a clear plastic pack.

"Oh joy.   Just what I've always wanted," he said, pouting. "Thank you."

"Okay, who's next?" Marilyn asked cheerfully.

"Well, it just so happens that I have number two," Darius began.

"Here it comes," Austin said. "A speech."

"*Ahem.*   Where was I before I was so rudely interrupted?" Darius feigned a moment of thought, his hand cradling his chin. "Ah yes, my selection. Though, on *one* hand, I'd like to extend the drama, perhaps selecting from the potential treasures in front of which lovely Rosie is now standing . . . "

Rosie curtsied in front of the tree wearing a green corduroy skirt and white blouse, holding the trash bag.

" . . . thereby raising the entertainment level by at least one notch as we may all bear further witness to the animated and delightful display of anguish by our number crunching cohort . . . I must also consider the risk."

Austin grinned. "Are you *done*?"

"Patience, dear friend, as I'm indeed drawing near to an end."

"Phew, thank *God*."

Darius slid from his stool. "Mr. Drew, you may now exercise my turn in exchange for the nickel wound prize that rests in your hand."

Austin sang the second verse of a Three Dog Night song about the number two.

"*Christ*," Harvey said, "how high does that song *go*?"

Josh shook his head, watching Drew prance back to the tree, his hands drawn under his chin like a dog begging for food.

This time Drew selected a small box, no doubt hoping to avoid further exertion. He opened it. "Oh *look*, a *scarf*!"

"I'll take that," Marilyn said, "you can have my next pick."

One by one, they each relieved Drew of his prize, sending him repeatedly to the tree. Retrieving each gift, he systematically removed bows and handed them to Marilyn, removed paper and delivered it to Rosie, then unwrapped each gift unquestionably intended for someone else. A songwriter's journal for Tom. A pair of lined work gloves for Rosie. A Macy's gift certificate for Annie. A collar and leash for Freddie, presumably for his stuffed monkey. A guitar stand for Josh. A copy of Dale Carnegie's 'How to Win Friends and Influence People' for Harvey. Photo editing software for Lech. Drumsticks for Austin. Drew opened the last gift from under the tree. A clown nose. He sighed with relief. "Oh, finally something I can *use*."

"I'll take that," Rex said.

Darius held a hand to his mouth while Austin looked around at snowflakes on the walls. Rosie collected the small folded papers from everyone around the room, each inscribed with the number one, and placed them into the garbage bag.

Drew's eyes travelled around the room. "*Oh! Oh!* A con*spir*acy!" He whined. "This was all *staged!*"

The group burst into fits of laughter at Drew's unintended pun and his realization of their coordinated prank.

Drew's lip quivered. "Josh?", he said, his voice cracking.

"I'm sorry, Drew. They outnumbered me."

Austin snickered.

Drew crossed his arms and plopped in a chair.

The toy train whistle blew.

"Drew?" Marilyn said softly, standing next to him. He looked up at a larger gift she held in her hand and wiped a tear from his cheek. Drew took the gift and unwrapped it slowly. A lighted mirror.

Rex cleared his throat, then rasped. "There were two more gifts." He waddled behind the couch, retrieving two medium sized, wrapped presents.

"This one just has Lech's name scribbled on it." Rex handed a gold wrapped gift to Lech.

"The other one is for Tom." Rex met Tom halfway.

Tom quizzically searched the faces around the room before unwrapping the gift and opening the box. He slowly lifted a wooden carousel, held it up and spun the fan gently, momentarily drawn to a wooden guitar player, mechanically strumming his hand and tapping his foot in the center.

Baker's Dozen

He pulled a note from inside the box. Someone sniffled as Tom read the note to himself.

Dear Tom,

I'm so sorry. I would never do anything to hurt you in a million years.

More than anything, I need to know if you care. I need to know that we have something together. But, I don't want to remind you of your loss. I can't bear that you'll look at me and think I'm responsible.

I care about you and I care about Freddie. Sadly, it hurts me to see Freddie with Annie. Yet, I honestly believe she fell between the cracks. I can see her heart and it is true. They deserve time together, without interference. You deserve time to heal. That's why I'm leaving.

When you receive this, I will be with my cousin in Santa Monica. She's the only real family I have left. If you want me to come back, I will. All you have to do is call me and I'll board the next plane. Please, let it be so. Please call me and let me know that you feel the same way about me that I feel about you. I love you no matter what happens. There, I said it. I do. I love you. For me, it's not about money. It's about people who matter. You matter.

Forever yours,

Janie

P.S.   My cousin's phone number is (310) 395-9700.

"It's from Janie," Tom said.   "How did this git here?"

Marilyn blew her nose on a napkin. "She asked that I give it to you,"

"How'd she git the money to go to Santa Monica?"

Drew and Josh exchanged glances.

"Well," Drew said, "I gave her an advance."

Rosie said, "How *dare* you write checks out of our business account!"

"It was authorized."

The train rattled around toward a handful of bows Freddie had placed on the tracks.

"Lech, aren't you gonna open your gift?" Drew asked.

Staring at his name in crooked letters across the attached tag, Lech shook his head. "Thank you everybody. I had fun." He leaned forward, retrieving his photo editing software from the floor in front of his chair then used an elbow to lift himself up. He moved toward the steps. "I'm kinda tired. Merry Christmas."

Wearing an aviator's fur lined hat and heavy coat, Harvey grunted as he lifted the final ninety-five pounds of snow with his shovel, tossing both snow and shovel into the road, then clapping his hands clean. Leaning down, he picked up a brown paper bag before rapping on the side of the van. "Who is it?" Gene's voice echoed from inside.

"It's Harvey."

A click, then the door squawked open. Francis' head appeared, his fedora pulled down low over his Ray Bans. "Whadd'ya want?"

"I brought hot chocolate and cranberry bread."

"Thanks." Francis' black jacketed arm hooked around the door and accepted the bag before retracting slowly into the van, pulling the door closed behind him.

CHAPTER THIRTY EIGHT

Drew squeezed the bulb of a horn mounted to a walker he frequently used as a prop at the children's oncology ward. *"Hoo, Honk!"*

Royce Jacobsen nearly jumped out of his dark gray, Glen plaid suit, seated with his back to the conference room door where Drew plopped and drug, plopped and drug.

In his tights and tutu, the skinny clown hobbled around the table, stopping a few times to honk the horn on the walker, followed by Rex, also in full costume, pretending to push. Rex pulled a chair out from the table, following Drew's butt as he weaved from side to side, having parked his walker near the wall. As Drew began to sit, Rex moved the chair, anticipating the skinny clown's next move to the other side. Drew landed on the floor, then his head popped up again, at the same level as Rex, just above the table, two clown faces staring at the executive, at each other, then again at Jacobsen.

"For some reason," Harv's voice echoed down the corridor, "I woke up this morning wanting to kill my whole family."

"That's what happens when you drink a gallon of vodka," Rosie's voice echoed in response.

Jacobsen turned as Rosie appeared next to Harvey's enormous hairy chest partially draped in overalls, standing outside the doorway, his head obscured. Harvey bent at the waist, then followed Rosie through the door to the opposite side of the table where Rex and Drew were now seated. Rosie wore faded jeans and a red and black checked flannel shirt tied at her midriff, revealing her tight abdominal muscles. She plopped down into a chair, then slumped, scowling at the executive. Harvey sat next to her, picking his teeth with a large hunting knife, his head turned toward Rosie, but his eyes angled at Jacobsen.

"*Boo!*" Harvey shouted. Jacobsen jumped again.

"*Ha!*" Harvey grinned, tilting the tip of the hunting knife toward the man. "Gotcha!"

Voices sang the harmony to a familiar song from down the hall. Darius, Tom and Austin filed into the room, sitting at the opposite end of the table on the same side as Jacobsen. Austin drummed the table with his fingers. Tom mouthed rhythmic onomatopoeia as Darius rapped the lyrics to 'Rapture.'

As Jacobsen handed out a few business cards, a scuffling noise drew his attention to the carpet at the door. Ben scurried to the front of the room, tethered at the end of a leash held by Freddie, who stood inches away, staring down at the exec.

Jacobsen put a hand over his eyes, inhaling and exhaling deeply.

"Freddie, please give Mr. Jacobsen some room," Josh's voice came from the opening, closing the door gently behind him. He side stepped around Freddie and Ben at the end of the table then sat between Rosie and Rex on the other side.

Jacobsen peeked between his fingers as Freddie pulled a slice of bologna from his pocket and bent, feeding the meat to the rat, who waddled under the table. Freddie plopped in a chair in the corner.

The door creaked open. "Sorry, I'm late." Marilyn shuffled in house slippers to the open chair between Darius and Mr. Jacobsen.

Ben gnawed and smacked from beneath the table.

Josh squeaked in his chair. "Mr. Jacobsen?"

"Oh, I'm, uh." His mouth still open, Jacobsen had turned to hand out another business card, but sat paralyzed with his arm extended, staring at Marilyn. She smiled demurely.

"I'm sorry," he stammered, "I, uh, have we met?"

"I don't think so," she said, taking his card.

Jacobsen shook his head, astonished, maintaining his gaze.

Angling her sparkling blue eyes at Josh, Marilyn put two fingers to her full lips, blushing.

"I'm sorry," the exec continued. "I'm just trying to figure it out."

"What do you mean?" Josh asked.

"I mean. Well. She's so . . . ," his voice trailed.

"Normal," Darius said.

"Yes."

Everyone at the table laughed except Freddie and Mr. Jacobsen.

Josh cleared his throat and squeaked forward, his arms resting on the table. "What brings you here today, Mr. Jacobsen?"

"Yes, well, thank you for letting me visit with you today."

Mr. Jacobsen fidgeted in his seat.

"Yes?"

"I'm sorry, I lost my train of thought."

"You were thanking us for having you here."

"Yes. Right. I want to commend you for making such a splash in the marketplace."

The executive fidgeted again.

Austin drummed his fingers on the table. Darius hummed something.

Jacobsen pushed his chair back and peered under the table.

"*Jesus Christ*! That rat's chewing on my new Ferragamo's!"

Darius displayed his Buckwheat face.

"Pardon me, Roy," Austin sang, "is that the rat-that-chewed-your-new-shoes?"

Josh shook his head, then motioned toward the door with his fingers. "Freddie, please take Ben outside."

"Okkkaaaaayyyyyyyyy!" Freddie whined. "C'mon Ben." Freddie stood and coaxed Ben with a slice of American cheese, also retrieved from his pocket.

The door clicked behind them. Jacobsen inhaled and exhaled loudly.

"I'm sorry about that," Josh said. "We really should think about getting Freddie a kitten. You were saying?"

Jacobsen lowered his head for a moment, trying to regain his composure. "Magma is prepared to make an offer," he said quietly.

"No thanks, Mr. Jacobsen, I already have a job."

"You don't understand. We're prepared to acquire . . . I'm sorry . . . what do you call yourselves again?"

Josh said, "Baker Electronics."

"Right." Jacobsen leaned down and lifted a leather satchel onto his lap, pulling out a sheet of paper and sliding it across the table.

"What"s this?" Josh asked.

"It's an offer."

Josh sighed, then began reading. "Hmmmm," he said, pursing his lips. He slid the paper down to Rex. "We'll make that much this quarter," Josh said quietly.

"Excuse me?"

"We'll net out this amount," Josh extended his left hand and tapped the page in front of Rex, "by the end of March."

Jacobsen's jaw tightened. He pulled a tablet from the satchel, then leaned to put the leather case back on the floor. He sniffed loudly. "I'd like to show you something," he said.

Jacobsen tapped the screen a few times then turned it for Josh to see. "This is our virtual mixer system." He slid his finger across, advancing to the next slide. "It does everything that your system does . . . and more."

Rex knitted his eyebrows and said with a rasp, "You don't have the data."

"Oh, yes, but we *do*."

Josh leaned back and folded his hands under his chin. "We spent years collecting data," he said. "There's no way."

"Ah, Mr. Baker. You'd be surprised. We have a lot of resources at our disposal."

Josh exhaled loudly.

Jacobsen continued. "Like yours, our system has a feedback system, but we also have a small peripheral that'll plug into each amplifier, automatically generating a signal."

Rex stood in his chair then climbed onto the table, his fists clenched at both sides of the round hoop supporting his checked pants. "That's our design and you know it!"

"Rex! No!" Josh held his hand up. "Let him finish."

"There's not much else to say other than we'll beat you," Jacobsen said.

Josh cleared his throat. "We've submitted our patent application," he said.

"Do you know how many patent cases we've won over the years? You don't have a chance," Jacobsen sneered. He lifted the tablet from the table. "We've got the best patent attorneys in the industry, just ask anyone."

"But," Josh began, "we can show prior art and how our system's different."

"Yes, but our's was developed at the same time. By the way, your system is now obsolete."

"Mister!" Austin shouted from the end of the table, "You've gotta lotta nerve!"

Jacobsen slid the tablet into his attache'. "I've been doing this a long time. You've missed your opportunity."

"We've beaten you to the market," Darius said.

The executive said, "What you fail to understand is that we carry a lot of weight in this industry. Nobody in their right mind will risk losing us, especially when we now have the superior product."

Jacobsen, standing, opened the door. He paused, taking stock of Josh and his employees. "Next time, Mr. Baker, you may want to align yourself more carefully with a better group of people."

CHAPTER THIRTY NINE

Darius knocked lightly on Josh's open door and peeked in. "How's it goin' boss?"

"Not great." Josh replied. "C'mon in."

Darius waved at Freddie, playing with his monkey on the floor. "Hey, Freddie. Have you seen Tom?"

"He went to the airport to pick up Janie," Freddie answered without looking up.

"Oh, really?" Darius lowered himself into a chair and folded his hands, nodding with an 'I-just-bit-into-a-green-persimmon,' look on his face, studying the top of Josh's desk. "What's all *this* stuff?"

"You'll like this." Josh lifted a letter. "This one's from the EPA." He laid it upside down in a stack, then lifted another letter. "This one's from the City of Chicago, citing a number of violations. A few might actually be legit."

"Such as?"

"We've complied with most of the permit violations, but they suspect we're operating a food truck."

"*Naw!*" Darius forced a smile, trying to break the tension. "Where on *earth* do they come up with such things?"

Josh scattered a stack of letters on the surface of his desk. "Just take your pick," he said. He closed his eyes, waving his finger in a circle before dropping it straight down. "Here's one directly to me from someone who hates rich people. On paper, maybe. Oh, and *this* one. This one's scary. It's from The Anarchist State Solidarity Society."

"Isn't that a contradiction in terms?" Darius said.

"I'm not gonna tell 'em."

Darius asked, "What does it say?"

Josh read for a minute then laughed. "Apparently, we're wealthy industrialists."

"*What?*"

Josh shrugged his shoulders. "I guess we're an easier target for them."

"Here's one from Most Holy Church," Josh continued. "We're all going to hell. The IRS wants an audit. Developers want to buy our property. The State of Illinois. OSHA."

"OSHA?" Darius said. "*Really?*"

Josh read the letter. "We're on their watch list. Apparently, an anonymous caller tipped them off. Meanwhile, sales are lagging."

"*Josh!*" a familiar voice called from the door.

Janie dropped her bag and ran across the office, meeting Josh at the corner of his desk, hugging him.

"I *missed* you," she said.

"Me too."

"Look who da *cat* done drug in," Darius said, extending his arms for a hug.

"Tom told me about Magma," Janie said. "That's just *aw*ful."

"Yeah, they're leaning pretty hard on us," Josh said, "but we'll be okay."

"*Freddie!*" Janie ran to where Freddie sat on the floor and knelt beside him. "How *are* you?"

"You left," Freddie mumbled.

"I'm sorry, Freddie. But look, I came *back*." Janie held her arms wide, then hugged as Freddie leaned away from her.

Josh's phone rang. "It's my dad."

"C'mon, let's go downstairs to see everybody," Janie said, standing.

"I wanna stay with Josh," Freddie said.

Josh nodded and waved them on.

Josh said, "Hi dad." He sat in his chair, swiveling back and forth. "I don't think I can do this anymore," he said in a low voice.

Freddie rose to his feet.

Josh swiveled away from him. "Just getting a lot of heat."

Freddie dug his hand into his pocket, then tapped Josh on the shoulder. Josh held up a finger without looking. "Okay dad. Love you. Bye."

Josh leaned over his desk and put his face in his open hands. Freddie tapped him on the shoulder again.

"I'm sorry, Freddie," Josh mumbled. "What is it?"

"Here."

Josh peeked out from his hands. Freddie held a fresh $100 bill folded in half. "I can't take that, Freddie. It's going to be okay, I promise."

"Take it."

Josh sighed. With a half smile, he lifted his head and accepted the bill from Freddie, folding it out, running his finger across the blue seal of a crisp, $100 silver certificate, printed in 1928.

Josh's smile faded. "Freddie. Where did you get this?"

"Downstairs, in the basement."

CHAPTER FORTY

Freddie stood on his toes, pointing at a space over the partially collapsed ceiling. "Up there."

Josh climbed an aluminum step ladder, shining his flashlight into the space. "Through this air vent?" he asked.

"Yes," Freddie said.

"Is there a big space on the other side?"

"Yes."

Josh stepped down and put a hand on Freddie's shoulder.

"Freddie, please don't climb up there again, the rest of the ceiling could fall."

"Okay."

Josh shined the light along the top of the wall, then down the bricks in the dimly lit space.

Poink. "Where's that dripping noise coming from?" Josh wondered aloud.

He traced a line on the wall with his hand, to the left, down, to the right, down, stooping, then continuing to the bottom. "There's a seam in the bricks," he said. Using his finger, he scratched several inches of dirt away from the floor, then felt along the bottom of the wall where several bricks

227

were missing.   Josh pointed at the table on the other side of the room. "Hand me that stick."

Freddie grabbed the stick and placed it into Josh's open hand.

"*What's this*?" Josh inspected the leather riding crop, then shook his head. He used the butt end of the crop to scratch away years of accumulated dust and sediment from the recessed portion of the floor near the wall. "There's a rail."

Pressing one hand on the wall, Freddie leaned over him, inspecting the area to where Josh aimed the flashlight.

"We're gonna need more light and some help," Josh said.

Rex turned on a halogen light mounted on a portable stand. Josh turned his eyes away, holding the riding crop up in the intense light.   "Anybody know anything about this?"

Rex said, "That's mine." He waddled over and grabbed it.

"*Pervert*," Harv said.

Rex slapped the crop against his stumpy hand. "Keep shoveling or I'll smack *you* with it."

"Oh, *baby*!" Harv teased.

"I uncovered part of a rail," Josh said. "I think it goes further back."

Harv leaned down and swiped a finger on the exposed track. "Good thing it's greased."

Drew giggled. "I know. Don't *even* go there."

Josh stood and inspected the wall at chest level, occasionally scratching along the grout line between the bricks with Harv's hunting knife. "Here's something." Josh worked the knife around the perimeter of a brick, prying the loose brick forward until it fell into his hand. He tilted his head to look inside.

"What *is* it?" Rex asked.

"It's a clevis."

"What's a clevis?" Drew asked.

"It's like a big steel ring." Josh walked out of the light toward the opposite wall, shining his flashlight high. "I think I know why it's there."

Rex said, "Yes?"

"These bolts once held a winch." Josh pointed the light at several rusty bolts protruding through the wall.

Harv rested on his shovel. "Now you're talkin' *my* language."

Josh sighed, rubbing the back of his hand over his forehead.

"Hey, it's okay when *they* talk dirty," Harv whined, pointing at Rex and Drew.

"I think I get it," Drew said. "This was a *torture* chamber."

Rex swatted Drew on the butt with the riding crop. "Idiot! The winch was used to pull out a section of the wall."

Harv grinned at Drew. "How *was* it?" he asked.

Drew rubbed his butt. "Actually, not that bad. Kinda tingly."

Josh clicked off his flashlight. "We need a new winch."

CHAPTER FORTY ONE

Francis bunched his lips into an exaggerated smirk. "You ever wonder what could've been?"

"Yeah."

Francis looked over his Ray Bans. "I mean, what're we *doin'*?"

"Yeah."

Gene scratched under his hat.

Francis used his forefinger to push his glasses up on his nose. They sat on five gallon buckets in the back of the van, watching the monitor.

Gene said, "I always dreamed of installing swimming pools."

"We live in Chicago."

"Exactly."

Francis twisted the eraser end of a pencil in his ear. He said, "I could go back and finish school." He pulled the pencil out of his ear, inspecting the end.

"You dropped out at the beginning of the sixth grade," Gene said.

"Yeah, the year I turned eighteen."

"You can't go back."

"Exactly."

CHAPTER FORTY TWO

Ice had begun to melt in the center of the Chicago River. Steam rose then dissipated into the gray sky from an old warehouse building across the water.

"They're not payin' union scale," Jacobsen said, standing alone in his office, wearing a wireless.

"Nope," he said. "Talk to the woman." He sat on the edge of his desk, admiring a reproduction of a Matisse painting which hung above his credenza. "Right."

Someone tapped lightly on the door. Jacobsen pressed a button on his cell. "C'mon in!" he said, pressing the button again.

Nordstrom appeared, then turned to push the door slowly behind him until it clicked. He stood erect, waiting with his hands folded behind him.

Jacobsen swept his arm slowly across, oscillating his hand as though encouraging a small animal to walk. Nordstrom acknowledged with a tilt of his head, then found a space on a tan leather couch arranged with matching chairs at the opposite end of the office.

"Let me know." Jacobsen pressed a button. "So, what did they say?"

Nordstrom thumbed through a trade magazine, sitting straight.

"Nordstrom?"

"Oh. I'm sorry," Nordstrom replied. "I didn't realize you were talking to me." He placed the magazine carefully on a glass coffee table.

Jacobsen sighed. "What did they say?"

"They said that it'll never see the inside of a courtroom."

"Excellent."

CHAPTER FORTY THREE

Lech panned the camera around the room, the REC light flashing red in the top right corner. Darius and Austin stacked bricks they'd removed from the floor against the wall. They'd uncovered two rails below floor level, running half the length of the room. Rex brushed the remaining dirt and debris away from the rails with a whisk broom.

Harvey leaned on his shovel, wiping his brow with a red bandana. Drew held the stepladder while Josh balanced himself near the top, tightening the bolts on a new cable winch, mounted on the wall. Freddie played with his monkey, sitting on the table.

Josh stepped down, pulling the end of a steel braided cable with a hook mounted at the end. He clicked the cable across the room, then attached the hook to the large clevis.

"We need to take this really slow," Josh said. "It might take some prying near the wall to move this thing."

"I'll do the honors," Harv said, now standing on the bottom rung of the ladder. He glared at Drew and said, "Don't you get any ideas!" Drew held up both hands. Harvey climbed and braced himself, ready to turn the crank mounted on the side of the hand winch.

"Please be careful," Janie said. Lech panned to the three women who were sitting and watching from the steps. Marilyn and Annie waved at the camera.

"Okay, showtime," Lech said in a low voice.

"Harvey," Josh began, "you maintain the tension in the cable, but not too much at one time."

The winch clicked rapidly at first, the cable lifting from the floor into a straight line across the room. "*Stop!*" Josh checked the cable and used the flashlight to look at the clevis. "Okay guys, use your pry bars at the seam of the bricks to help when Harvey pulls."

Darius and Austin inserted the wedge end of their cheater bars into the cracks that had been cleared of dirt and moss. Darius wiggled his bar, gaining leverage.

"Not too much at one time. If we apply a balanced force, maybe we can move this thing," Josh said. "Okay Harvey, one click at a time."

Click.

"Again."

Click. The cable vibrated like a giant, bass guitar string.

Click. A short grinding sound echoed on the other side of the wall.

"It moved," Austin said, inspecting the eighth inch ledge created between the bricks on the stationary wall and the bricks mounted on the rail cart.

Austin adjusted his bar.

"Again."

Click.

Bricks ground against bricks as the cart shifted.

CHAPTER FORTY FOUR

"The new lofts will have an indoor pool and sauna."

Don Jackson, Alderman for the 27th Ward, admired the computer rendering of the converted warehouse space. He slid his finger across the screen, revealing another computer generated image with an expressionless man and woman walking along brick walks, winding through natural areas planted with trees. The Alderman's chair creaked. "When do you begin work?"

The architect cleared his throat. "Well, we have one little obstacle."

CHAPTER FORTY FIVE

REC flashed in the top right corner of the viewfinder, through which Lech viewed a section of brick wall mounted on a cart, now resting at the end of the track in the center of the room. It had moved easier with each successive click of the winch. Behind the cart, standing at the opening, Josh shined his flashlight around the inside of the tomb. *Poink!* A droplet echoed through the dark tunnel, from which a light, musty breeze emanated.

"Hand me the portable light," Josh said, reaching behind. Shadows danced around the room as Rex delivered the light stand to Josh's hand. The glow followed the halogen lamp through the thick wall into the space, leaving the group in relative darkness.

Lech stepped closer to the opening, his camera trained on the surrounding arched, brick lined tunnel where Josh now stood. "Wow," Josh said, looking up and over his head. He motioned to the camera, "Come with me."

The filmmaker weaved between the cart and Harv, then stepped through the opening into the tunnel where Josh lifted an old milk bottle from the floor with his fingers. "Not exactly what you'd expect to find in here," he said, releasing the bottle which clinked on the floor, off camera.

Stepping around Josh, Lech walked further into the tunnel, his long shadow leading the way. One hundred yards down the passage, a pale light originated from the right, casting a faint oval shape against the left wall. "It must be an old storm sewer," Josh's voice echoed from behind.

"Yuck."

"The floor's dry." Josh continued. "I don't think it's been in use for a long time."

"That's good."

Josh placed the halogen stand on the ground, then clicked his flashlight, providing additional light to a dark area of the wall directly to the left. A short passage -- also arched -- ended abruptly, only ten feet from where they stood together. Shining the flashlight down at their feet, a short wall separated the main tunnel from the inset. "What is it?" Lech voice echoed off camera.

"I think it's a dam to prevent water from getting through," Josh said.

Josh stepped over the short wall, moving slowly to the end of the space, shining his light along the floor, then up a brown scaly wall. Reaching out, he flaked a piece of the wall into his hand. "Rust."

"What do you think is behind the wall?" Lech asked.

"I think it's a vault." Josh ran his fingers over a lump. "Here's a hinge to a door." Josh pointed to another smaller protrusion. "I think this must be a latch. Harv will need an acetylene torch."

"Freddie," Josh's voice echoed through the tunnel. "Please come inside with us."

Freddie's head appeared on the other side of the opening. He stepped carefully into the space.

Josh asked, "Where'd you find the money?"

"Here." Josh followed Freddie's hand with the flashlight as he reached up into a hole where bricks had been removed from one side of the short tunnel. He pulled out an old leather satchel, then lifted a mildewed flap. Josh shined his flashlight at a stack of silver certificates.

CHAPTER FORTY SIX

Reaching the top of the stairs, ahead of the girls, Josh waved at Tom who threw his arms in the air, "Where's everybody *been*?"

"On a treasure hunt," Janie said, stepping around and planting a kiss on his cheek.

"How'd *that* work out?" Tom asked.

"Pretty good," Josh said, lifting the satchel. "There's probably thirty thousand in here."

"I don't believe you." Tom grinned, his eyes searching the others for clues.

Josh said, "Look for yourself."

Tom checked their faces again, then accepted the bag. He lifted the flap and pulled it open. "*Jesus*! Where'd you *foind* it?"

Josh pointed at Freddie. "Freddie found it. There's a hidden tunnel in the basement."

"Holy *cow*!" Tom said.

"We're gonna grab a bite to eat and rest for a bit," Josh said, placing his hand on the satchel. He grasped the bag and pulled gently. Tom held it against his chest, resisting. Josh tugged. Tom slightly twisted his body in opposition before releasing it, smiling.

Josh said, "I'll put this in the safe."

CHAPTER FORTY SEVEN

"Joshua Baker is evil!" a man wearing an Anarchist Solidarity State Society sweatshirt yelled over a bullhorn at Randolph and Halsted.

A woman passed flyers for A.S.S.S. to several dozen onlookers.

Across the street, a man in a suit emerged from inside an old warehouse converted to office condos. He stood for a moment, assessing the crowd, then crossed to where the woman passed flyers. He cleared his throat and she turned. "I'm just curious," he asked. "How much are they paying *you*?"

"I'm a volunteer," she said, offering a flyer. "Here, you can learn more about us."

"No, thank you." The man tossed his hand dismissively then turned and wandered back across the road.

"He's rich!" the man squawked through the bullhorn. The crowd booed. "He's taking advantage of the people!" The crowd booed again. "Are we gonna allow this to happen?"

"Noooo!" the crowd responded.

"Then, take one of these signs and walk with me!"

CHAPTER FORTY EIGHT

Lech watched Harvey through the viewfinder, REC flashing in the corner.

Ffffffffffffttttttttttttt! Harvey turned a knob on the lit blow torch until it popped out. He slid his green goggles onto his head and tapped the steel door with a welder's hammer. "Almost there," he said. "Couple more cuts oughta do it."

"Good," Josh's voice said from behind Lech.

Lech turned the camera with a mounted light shining into the larger tunnel where Josh stood. "I think you should say a few things," Lech said off camera.

"Well," Josh began, "I don't know."

"Just say what's on your mind."

Josh chuckled. "I'm not good at this sort of thing. I think Darius makes a better spokesperson."

Darius tilted his grinning face in front of Josh, wearing his backward cabbie's hat.

"Okay," Lech said. "So, Darius, what do *you* think?"

Josh stepped to the side, allowing Darius to straighten himself in front of the camera.

Del Boland

"You ask me what I think," Darius said, his eyes wide. "I think somebody was tryin' to *hide* somethin'!"

Josh laughed off camera.

"Why do you say that?"

"Well, a whole lotta work went into this. Either we're about to find the skeletal remains of somebody's crazy *sister*, or, we're about to make a significant discovery."

Harvey's voice shouted from off camera. "Somebody help me with this *door*."

Josh passed behind Darius, who glanced in the direction of Harvey. Darius turned and looked again at the camera. "Let's go see," he said. He spun ninety degrees and walked abruptly out of view, his upper body angled back as though following his feet forward.

Lech held the camera steady, focused on the background, capturing Austin's silhouette passing through the wall from the basement. "What's going on?" Austin asked.

"They're removing the door," Lech answered.

The camera followed Austin to where he stopped at the mouth of the shorter tunnel. Beyond Austin, Josh and Harvey shuffled together, carrying the steel door back several feet, then allowed it to clank against the wall. "Lech," Josh said, motioning with his hand. "Follow me in with the camera."

Lech sidestepped around Austin, then followed Josh and Harv through the corroded steel wall into

244

a blanket of cobwebs forming a silky cocoon around the partially obscured contents of the small space.

"Look at this," Josh said, pointing his flashlight and waving away cobwebs surrounding several wooden crates with empty milk bottles, stacked on the floor.

The spotlight from the camera followed Josh's flashlight beam to the back of the space, crisscrossing over the entombed objects. With one arm, Josh swam through, stepping around an old wooden desk, flanked by ghostly file cabinets against the rear wall. Lech panned the camera to a machine shop calendar hanging between the cabinets. He waved away the cobwebs, revealing a yellowed page from May 1931 curled at the edges, waiting for June.

Harvey waved his hand over, then opened the top drawer of one of the file cabinets. He reached inside and lifted a file folder.

"What is it?" Lech asked.

"Old manuals for machines." Harv opened another drawer.

Lech panned back to Josh who swept his arm over, clearing the space, then pressed his hand against a wooden chair, testing it's strength. He wiped the seat.

"Hey, look at this," Harv said off camera. Lech turned the camera back toward Harvey holding up a dusty violin case. He laid it on the dusty desk. "Maybe it's a Stratocaster," he said.

Josh laughed, now seated at the desk. "You mean a Stradivarius."

"That's what I said."

Harvey pinned his flashlight between one shoulder and his face and flipped down the hasps, opening the back of the case toward the camera. "Would ya look at *that*."

Lech stepped around, angling the camera down. A Thompson machine gun lay in pieces, carefully arranged inside the molded case. "Wow," Lech said.

Harvey lifted the drum magazine and examined it. He said, "This is a piece of history."

Lech went back to Josh who'd slid the top drawer open. He pushed the empty drawer back into the desk then reached down, tugging at the bottom file drawer until the dry-rotted wood splintered. "So much for that lock," he said, dragging the larger drawer open.

"Now we know what they were hiding," Harvey said to Darius and Austin off camera.

"What is it?" Austin asked from behind Lech.

Josh held up a paper bound stack in front of the camera. "One hundred dollar bills."

Darius edged around Lech, in view of the camera, then leaned over and whispered something in Josh's ear. Josh nodded.

CHAPTER FORTY NINE

"Deb, what's going on down there?"

"Hi Jim. A crowd has gathered outside of Baker Electronics directly behind me. Lou, if you can get a shot,"

The camera moved to the left, passing over a crowd holding signs.

"As you can see, many of the protesters are holding signs. 'FAIR WAGES FROM MILLIONAIRE BAKER,' 'UNSAFE WORKING CONDITIONS AT BAKER ELECTRONICS,' and one sign that simply reads, 'ANARCHY'. These are just a few of the messages.

The camera turned back to Deb holding her mike with one gloved hand in front of a protester. "Why are you here?", she asked a heavily bearded man wearing a Bears coat and matching knit cap.

"Baker Electronics is a sweat shop. They have autistic kids working without pay and the conditions are deplorable."

"Hunh?!" Darius yelled at the television screen. "Ask 'em where they got the information! What ever happened to checking the *facts*!"

"I say we go out there," Harv said.

"*I'll keep you posted with further developments*," Deb's voice said.

Darius muted the volume with a remote.

"I agree with Harv," Janie said.

"Wait a minute," Darius said. "You agree with *Harvey*? You feelin' okay?"

Rex said, "I agree with him, too."

"Okay," Darius said. "Now it's gettin' *really* freaky in here. Maybe it's all about to end."

"The business?" Austin asked.

"*Naw*," Darius replied. "I mean the world as we *know* it. This is *crazy*, dawg. Rex and Janie agreein' with Harvey. Television reporters who don't ask tough questions. How did we end up on everyone's radar? That's what *I* wanna know."

A helicopter hovered over the warehouse.

An auburn haired woman in her 30's faced a camera with a light shining on her face. "Jim, a group of people just arrived from inside the building, presumably to confront the protesters. Chicago Police are on hand to maintain order, but tempers are flaring."

The newswoman moved toward Darius and Austin, standing at the front of the group. "Sir, what can you tell me about Joshua Baker?"

Darius looked around at the crowd, then at the camera. He opened his mouth to speak, but nothing came out. He glanced at the crowd again and muttered, "No comment."

Austin raised his eyebrows and turned to his friend. Darius shrugged his shoulders.

Deb shifted her position along the front, holding one gloved hand to her ear. "I'm now standing with one of the employees of Baker Electronics. What's your name?"

"Rosie."

"Rosie, can you tell me a little about your life on the inside of that building?"

"I don't understand all of this. We're treated really . . . " several yelling protesters rendered Rosie's voice unintelligible. Deb hurriedly moved to where Chicago police had placed handcuffs on Josh.

"I'm told that Josh Baker, CEO and President of Baker Electronics, has been arrested." The camera located one of the police officers. "Sir," Deb began, "can you tell me the charges filed against Mr. Baker?"

"No, I cannot."

The camera returned to Deb who listened as someone spoke to her from off camera.

"I don't have confirmation, but I'm told that Mr. Baker has been arrested on several permit violations. Wait a minute." Someone else spoke from off camera. "Jim, I'm also told that an IRS agent just now issued an order for Baker Electronics to close until an audit can be conducted."

CHAPTER FIFTY

From his elevated position behind the bench, the judge peered over his half rim glasses at Josh and his attorney. Waving an ink pen, he spoke to the attorney. "Jim, where do you find these guys?"

Jim, the attorney, smiled and shrugged.

The judge said, "Are we still on for Saturday?"

Jim nodded.

"Let's get this over with," the judge said. He shuffled a few papers. He said, "In the case of 53117, City of Chicago vs. Baker, how do you plea?"

"My client pleads guilty, your honor," Jim said.

Rap! The judge said, "Defendant pay the court clerk $1,500."

The judge continued. "In the case of 53118, City of Chicago vs. Baker, how do you plea?"

"My client pleads guilty, your honor," Jim said again.

Rap! "Defendant pay the court clerk $2,500."

"In the case of 53119, City of Chicago vs. Baker, how do you plea?"

"My client pleads guilty, your honor."

Rap! "Defendant pay the court clerk $2,000."

."In the case of 53120, City of Chicago vs. Baker, how do you plea?"

"My client pleads guilty, your honor."

Rap! "Defendant pay the court clerk $1,500. Upon payment of all your fines, Mr. Baker, you will be free to go."

Josh shook his attorney's hand. "Nice work, counselor."

"Thanks."

Rex had followed Josh and the Bailiff down a hallway to the City Clerk's office. The little man pulled a roll of cash from his pocket to pay Josh's fines.

"I'm tellin' ya, Josh. I could have done a better job than that. I could'a fixed it up for ya."

Josh looked down at his feet. "Thanks, but no thanks," he replied.

"What about the IRS thing?" Rex asked.

"Apparently, we have a problem with our tax returns. I need to speak with Drew."

Across the desk, the clerk tapped a keyboard. A sheet of paper wiggled out of a nearby printer, then dropped. The clerk handed the receipt across to Rex.

Rex tugged at the massive door, stepping backward, then held it for Josh, following him into the massive corridor.

"Uh. About that," Rex said.

"What?" Josh replied.

"Drew's gone. Flew the coop. Hit the road."

"When?"

Rex sighed. "After the IRS issued the order," he said.

"Hmmmmm," Josh said.

"Yes, hmmmmm, indeed. I think he's been skimming." Rex opened another door leading outside. "What were all those charges?" Rex asked, following Josh across the portico into the sunlight.

Josh smirked, then said, "Operating a food truck without a permit."

Rex said, "I'm the one operating the food truck."

"Yes, but, it's in my name."

"Sorry, Josh."

"Violation of zoning for a residential facility," Josh continued, casually descending granite steps.

"You don't charge us."

"Doesn't matter," Josh said. "We're not zoned residential, period. Mostly code violations."

Rex hopped alongside Josh to keep up. "Wow. Who tipped them off?"

"I don't know. Probably Jacobsen." Josh stepped onto the sidewalk in front of the courthouse.

Rex followed. "How much did the attorney cost?"

"Five grand, but he says he gets a break on the fines."

Rex said, "That's some damn fine lawyering."

"Yeah."

CHAPTER FIFTY ONE

"Mommy, is that the Easter Bunny?" a little boy asked.

"Um. I think so." The mother scrunched her mouth to one side, assessing the slender woman in a short pink skirt and a white lycra, sleeveless top.

Marilyn wore furry, white bunny ears with pink satin on the inside. She handed the grinning boy a light blue helium balloon and a multi-colored woven basket from a cardboard box just inside the door. "There's eggs hidden all around," Marilyn said. "Some with a special prize inside."

The woman pulled the smiling, waving boy by the hand toward a line of kids waiting for free ice cream at a food truck.

"Nice work, *toots*," Rex said from behind.

"You're a lovely person, but I must admit, you make me a little uncomfortable sometimes," Marilyn said, tugging at the hem of her skirt.

Rex grinned up at her with his newly painted expression -- a happy clown face. "It's not my fault that you're so tall."

"How're you holding up?" she asked.

Baker's Dozen

"I'm okay. Had to change my routine. You have any idea how hard it is to do solo as a clown?"

Marilyn shook her head. "I must say, you look happier."

"Yeah, thought I'd change it up a little. Besides, Josh doesn't want me scarin' the kids."

"Hey!" Harv yelled from his position outside the garage opening, wearing a white tux and a pink bow tie. "Back away from the *bunny*, pervert!" He aimed his finger like a pistol at Rex and squeezed off a round.

"You know, I heard they're making a sequel to The Goonies!," Rex shouted back. "You'd make an excellent Sloth!"

Harv straightened his bow tie. "You really *think* so?"

"*Yeah*! Just think of the *money* they'd save in *make*-up!"

"This is tha famous, or should I sye *infamous*, vault -- one of Mr. Capone's personal hideaways. Besides over $1.4 Million in newly minted silver certificates, we discovered purchase orders, work orders, invoices and pyroll for . . . " Tom waited a few seconds. "Can anyone guess what business?"

A high school aged boy with red hair raised his hand.

"Yes?" Tom asked.

"Liquor?" the boy replied.

"Very good guess, but the answer is milk. Al Capone discovered he could mike more money in the milk business."

"Okay, another question for ya," Tom began. "Do ya know who began puttin' expiration dites on milk?"

The same high schooler raised his hand. Tom nodded at him.

"Al Capone?"

"That answer is correct, young man. Yes, Al Capone is responsible for the now common practice of putting expiration dites on milk. Does anyone know what other notable contribution Capone mide?"

A middle aged woman said, "Soup kitchens."

"That, too, is correct. Mr. Capone -- before the St. Valentine's Day Massacre -- was considered a modern dye Robin Hood. He regularly handed out money to the poor. He started soup kitchens, some believe, to bolsta that image. Despite his choice of career, he obviously felt a certain moral obligition."

A man's familiar voice came from the back of the room. "Aren't you going a bit too far, professor?"

"Well, Mr. Tourist, sir," Tom chortled, "I'm just tryin' to offer a complate picture. You must decide for yourselves."

"Seems to me," Darius continued, standing in the center of the group, "Mr. Capone may have been under the impression that his good works might save him."

Tom nodded, smiling, "That might very well be true."

"What happened to all the money?" a short, heavy set man in a Hawaiian shirt asked.

"Good question," Tom answered. "We gyve it to the City of Chicago."

"Couldn't you keep it?"

"Actually no," Tom said. "The money was considered stolen propitty."

Darius said, "And how is it that you're able to preserve this fine example of free enterprise?"

Tom nodded his head. "Well, as ya all know, we're now a cultural centa, offering our spice to groups in addition to runnin' reg'lar tours."

Darius continued, "That hardly seems enough to maintain a space this size."

"Well, sir, in order to protect national landmarks in this country, you must sometimes resort to creative manes."

Darius chortled. "I think what our eloquent *tour* guide is trying to *say* is, in order to raise *money* for a landmark, you must first threaten to tear it *down*."

Several among the tour group chuckled.

"Thank you, Darius, for your insoits. Ladies and gentlemen, we'll roid back up the service elevator to the mine level whare you mye view many of the artifacts that were found in this room displayed insoid our museum gift shop."

Holding a little girl's hand, Lech leaned over and pointed up to stained glass windows all around the inside of the warehouse. Red, blue and green light reflected on all the surfaces inside the cavernous space. "It's so pretty in here," she said.

"Yes, it is. The light changes throughout the day, so it looks different every time you see it."

Josh puttered up on a flatbed Cushman cart and squeaked to a stop. He waved at the little girl who clutched her father's leg.

"Josh, this is my daughter, Aleska."

Josh slid across the seat of the cart in his beige coveralls. He planted one knee on the floor in front of the girl, taking her hand. "Ah, Aleska, defender of mankind. I'm very honored to meet you." He bowed his head and she curtsied.

"What are *they* doing?" she asked, pointing at Harv and Rosie, rolling out long wooden pews into the open space where families continued to mingle.

"We're getting ready for a show," Josh said. "Tonight, we're very fortunate to have The Fallow Wing performing right up there." Josh, still kneeling, turned and pointed at the mezzanine where truss lights and a large screen were visible.

Josh used one hand on his knee to lift himself. "Lech, may I please offer my apologies for all the innuendo?"

"It wasn't you."

"No," Josh said, "but I feel responsible nonetheless."

"Well, thank you," Lech replied. "Thank you for everything you've done for *all* of us."

"I'd like to give something to Aleska. That is, if you don't mind?"

"Nothing elaborate, please."

"No," Josh said. "Just a little something."

"Okay."

"Aleska," Josh said, "please come with me." Lech and his daughter followed Josh to a newly constructed retail space against the north wall. A bell tinkled as they entered. Janie waved from behind a display where she arranged The Fallow Wing's latest cd, 'Baker's Dozen,' on a shelf. "Hi Josh," Annie said from behind the cash register.

"Hi Annie. I'd like to present Miss Aleska with a very special gift today."

"Oh, how wonderful," Annie smiled.

"I'd like her to have the silver charm bracelet, please," Josh said, pointing inside of the glass case below the cash register.

Aleska put both hands to her face, her mouth and eyes open wide. "Oh, thank you so much!"

"Would you like me to wrap it for you?" Annie asked, retrieving the bracelet from the case.

Josh waited on a response from Aleska, who turned to Lech. "Daddy, may I wear it, *please*?"

"Of course," Lech said.

Annie stooped down and clasped the bracelet on the little girl's arm.

Lech said, "Thank you again."

"No worries," Josh replied. "We're friends."

Darius looked out across a sea of families, some standing together and others seated.

Austin twirled one drumstick in his left hand then another in his right. "You okay?" he asked.

"Yeah." Darius turned the volume down on his P bass then silently plucked a couple of notes for good measure. He said, "I'm not the one I'm worried about."

"We've been through it a million times with him," Austin said. "He'll be fine."

Darius lifted the strap of his bass over his head and ducked under, holding it by the neck to his side.

"Thank you very much," Josh said into the mike, smiling at the crowd. "Thank you all for coming out today. We'd like to close with a new song." Josh turned away from the microphone. "You okay back there?"

"We're fine," Darius hollered over his shoulder, placing the strap over Freddie's head. "Okay my man," Darius said to Freddie, "let's have some fun. Remember. Turn up the volume." Darius leaned down in Freddie's line of sight and slapped gently against the side of the young man's smiling face.

Freddie nodded, rolling the knurled knob in his fingers, feeling the travel, then resting at 70%.

"Ladies and Gentlemen," Josh said, "I'd like to introduce you to a talented young man, and a close personal friend, Freddie Funk, on bass guitar!"

"Woo hoo!" Rosie yelled and waved from the other side of the mezzanine.

A finger to her lips, Annie placed a gentle hand on Rosie's shoulder.

Janie shoved Darius playfully away then held Freddie by his shoulders. "Okay Freddie, I'll be right here," she said. "Remember what Tom said. Just feel the music and do what you like to do," her golden eyes glistening.

"Thank you," Freddie said.

Tom waved encouragement to Freddie from his position on the stage.

"Okay, let's do this," Josh said. "One, Two, ..."

BACK FROM CALIFORNIA
(Track 7)

Listen
and you will find
your pulse
in sync with mine
No one
can speak the truth
and make me believe

Del Boland

in myself like you do

I was weightless
up in space and
you pulled me down
and rescued me
I was hiding
undecided
and it all caught up with me
You were back from California
with one request to be free
"but this one is worth the wait"
kept ringing inside my head
and I said stop
this sounds too good to be true

The likeness of your kind
doesn't come around everyday
and the way deception is oblate
cause I know your real to me
and it lets me see
like a sixth sense
my defense is shed
I lay my head to rest
and I day dream of
the days and nights,
days and nights alone
with you

Baker's Dozen

Roadside, sitting on a wooden fence,
stricken by the daylight
thinking about the life
I want to live with you by my side
Somehow someway swept away,
like an anchorless boat
on a warm and windy summer day
and everything's ok

I know you didn't know it
but it took some time to show you
that I'd do no wrong
to you

Hey girl
its never been like this
My lips
long for your sweet kiss
My body
awaits you
while my soul sings about you
loneliness is dead

I was waking up from aching,
I was taking up some space
that day had rearranged
my life was changed

Del Boland

when I saw your face
I stopped sinking
started thinking
about you and me
in another place
but you kept a steady,
line you never
gonna let me cross

The likeness of your kind
doesn't come around everyday
and the way deception is oblate
cause I know your real to me
and it lets me see
like a sixth sense
my defense is shed
I lay my head to rest
and I day dream of
the days and nights,
days and nights alone
with you

Roadside, sitting on a wooden fence,
stricken by the daylight
thinking about the life
I want to live with you by my side
Somehow someway swept away,
like an anchorless boat

Baker's Dozen

on a warm and windy summer day
and everything's ok

CHAPTER FIFTY TWO

"Dad!" Josh waved down at a large man with a neatly trimmed white beard and sunglasses.

Josh reached for Marilyn's fingers dangling at her side. "C'mon, I want you to meet my father!"

Holding hands, they walked together down the steps, Marilyn's bunny ears swaying.

Josh and his father embraced, slapping each other on the back. Josh pushed himself away, then stood to the side, his hand on his father's shoulder.

"Marilyn, I'd like you to meet my father, Jordan Baker." Josh pointed his open hand, palm up, at his father's chest, then with a sweeping motion, he presented Marilyn. "Dad, this is Marilyn."

Mr. Baker the elder smiled warmly, enwrapping her slender hand into his large, protective mitts. "I've heard so much about you."

"And I, about you," Marilyn said, blushing. "Based on Josh's description, I was starting to believe that you didn't exist."

Jordan said, "I'm sorry. I've been very busy."

Josh faced his father. "It's okay, Dad. Let us show you around."

Marilyn tapped Josh on the shoulder. "Josh, there they *are*," she said in a low voice, tilting her head to one side.

Two men in fedoras watched from fifty feet away, the shorter man with a stoic expression standing with his arms folded and the taller man eating cotton candy.

"Oh, that's Gene and Francis," Josh's father said.

"You *know* them?" Josh asked.

Jordan waved them over. "They work for me." The two men approached. "Hi boys," Jordan said, "this is my son, Josh and his lovely . . . friend . . .," he smiled, " . . . Marilyn."

Both men touched their fedoras with a slight nod.

Marilyn giggled.

"What's so funny?" Josh asked.

"We were all thinking they were on a mission from *God*."

Gene and Francis looked at each other and shrugged.

"I'm so glad I got to meet your father."

Josh poured champagne into two glasses. "He's an amazing man," he said. Josh handed one glass to Marilyn and raised the other in a toast. "Here's to happy endings." They clinked their glasses together and sipped.

Josh said, "Rex rigged up a sound system for me. Is it okay if I turn it on?"

"Sure."

Josh lifted a remote from his dresser and pressed a button. Soft jazz music played through speakers mounted around his room.

"Shhhhhh! Everybody be quiet!" Darius whispered, his hand in the air. He pressed his ear back against the wall.

Marilyn asked, "What was that *noise*?"

"I suspect they're all in the next room listening in."

"Hmmmmm. They're weird." Marilyn swayed with the music, her eyes closed. "Josh?"

"Yes?"

"Do you know everything?" she asked.

"What do you mean?"

She opened her eyes, studying him from an angle. "You seem to know everything that goes on around here. It's a little . . . well . . . *scary* sometimes."

Josh tilted his head. "*Really*?" he asked.

She nodded.

He said, "No, I don't know everything."

Marilyn sipped then peeked at Josh over the rim of her glass, one of her bunny ears bent down.

"Is there something *wrong* with me?" she asked, looking into her glass to avoid his gaze, biting her lip.

"Absolutely not."

"I mean . . . you know . . . you haven't . . . ," her voice trailed off. She sipped her champagne.

Josh smiled and moved closer to her, slowly running his fingers lightly along her bare shoulder. Josh leaned forward with slitted eyes, his head tilted slightly. Marilyn leaned back a few inches away from him.

"How about your *dad*?" she asked. "Does *he* know everything?"

Josh smiled and shook his head gently, pursuing her. He kissed the lobe of her ear.

She said, "Well, you know how folks sometimes talk . . . ."

"What do they say?" he whispered, grazing his lips against her neck.

"That you're . . . you're . . . kinda perfect, and nice," Marilyn breathed.

"I don't want to disappoint you," Josh said softly, kissing the space above her collar bone.

She lifted her chin slightly and whispered, "What do you mean?"

"I'm far from perfect."

Marilyn inhaled then exhaled, deeply, slowly. "You coulda . . . fooled . . . me." She turned her face toward him.

"Here, use this," Austin whispered, handing an empty glass to Darius.

Darius slapped at the air between them, making a shushing face.

Janie giggled.

"That's it!" Darius whispered. "Everybody out!" They filed out of the conference room ahead of him. Darius paused for a moment to look around the conference room, then turned the light out.

CHAPTER FIFTY THREE

"And, they lived happily ever after." Jordan Baker looked at the three week old boy sleeping on his broad chest. "What a beautiful child."

"Thanks Dad," Marilyn said.

"You're welcome."

"I'll be glad when he's able to understand your stories," she said.

"Oh, you'd be surprised at what he understands," he said.

Marilyn laid her head on the old man's shoulder, her feet tucked under her on the sofa. "By the way, have I told you that you're a wonderful grandpa?"

"About a million times."

Marilyn yawned. "Sorry. Not getting much sleep."

"It's okay. You go ahead, I'll stay up with little Jordan for a while and put him to bed."

She stood and shuffled to the door. Stopping, she turned and said, "Nighty, night."

Josh said, "How's he doin'?"

"Great," Marilyn answered. "He's sleepin'."

"I meant the old man."

"Oh, he's been such a great help."

"Good."

Marilyn slipped under the covers and turned off the Tiffany lamp next to the bed.

"Last night, I had this crazy dream," she said in the darkness.

"What was it?"

She said, "If I told you, you wouldn't believe me."

"Try me."

"I dreamed you were, like, the Messiah, but nobody was talkin' about it."

"Jesus?" Josh said.

"Yes."

"How'd that turn out?"

"I was conflicted. Then you assured me that you were just an ordinary guy."

"Really?"

"Yeah," she said. "I thought I knew you. At least, I know you in real life."

"Okay," Josh said, smirking. "That's kinda weird, but I can see how you might think that about a guy like me."

Marilyn drifted for a moment. "Smarty," she murmured.

"So, how'd it end?"

"I dressed up like the Easter Bunny . . . ," she breathed slowly.

"Marilyn?"

Josh pulled the covers up and kissed her on the cheek.

"Sweet dreams."

FOOTPRINTS IN THE DIRT
(Track 10)

They can hardly contain their laughter
I don't care what they did last night
As you looked on they took what they were after
Won't you show them wrong from right
You can save the rest
It was all in jest
Now I stood by you
won't you stand by me today?

Your days are a maze in on this crazy living
No one knows whats at the end
Pick your side are you taking or giving
Your choice dictates what's around the bend
You can save your soul if you let it roll
Now I stood by you won't you hear me out today

When you leave your footprints in the dirt

Del Boland

Will they sing of love ?
Or scream of hurt ?
Will the lonely teardrops in your eyes
Leave dingy clouds in future skies?

Taking your shots at the undertaker
Fleeting thoughts now meandering
The mirror on the wall knows the truth within
you
Fooling us? Your the only fool

You can save the rest
It was all in jest
Now I stood by you
won't you stand by me today?

Craig Christiansen is a multi-talented musician, singer-songwriter, and music therapist from Chicago. He was featured on Wilco's award winning cd, 'Yankee Hotel Foxtrot."

Thanks to Craig for permission to include lyrics from his cd, also entitled 'Baker's Dozen.' Craig's socially conscious messages are integral to this story and listening to each track greatly enhances the reading experience, in my humble opinion. A portion of the net proceeds from the sale of this book will go to Craig's not-for-profit -- Creative Exchange Foundation -- benefitting special needs kids through music therapy in the Chicago area. In addition, I hope you'll help support Craig's foundation through direct purchase of his music on Amazon.com, or through the purchase of 'Baker's Dozen' on audiobook, soon to be released.

It was a great honor to be a part of GraceFlock -- a praise band at Christ Our Shepherd Lutheran Church in Peachtree City, GA. The experience resulted from a "God moment" in my life.

One Sunday, the band announced at the end of service that the previous bass player had moved and they needed a replacement. My lovely wife, Anne -- in her subtle way -- jabbed me in the ribs and shoved me toward the band. Having played guitar in a group for a few years, I meekly offered to help out and admitted, "No, I don't really play the bass . . . but I own one." The leader of the group said, "You're in." Two years later, I contributed to this recording, playing bass on most tracks and guitars on my original song, 'God Knows Everything,' the last track on the cd. 'Living Gifts' is a collection of 16 original songs that I hope will move and inspire you -- available on both CDBaby.com and Amazon.com. All proceeds benefit Lutheran World Relief.